Biblia Fabula

Stories of the Gospels

C. Rochelle Wilcox

J.J.

CONTENTS

MIDWIFE

When Zeer was finally able to go curl up in her corner, she was nearly too tired to sleep. There had never been such a day, and knowing that it was coming hadn't lessened the work of it. As soon as the decree had gone out, Fayvel started to lay in supplies as much as he was able--an extra jar of oil here, more flour there, an extra rope of garlic from the market. That way, when the first trickle of visitors began coming to Beit-Lechem, he was prepared to feed as many men as he had mats for in his upper room. And he had Zeer constantly working on weaving more mats. Weaving had been pleasant work for many days past with the clean straw in the open room, as she threaded in pungent grasses to keep the vermin away. And helping to organize the extra food in the kitchen had also been pleasant in its own way.   It was satisfying to see the stores of food grow. Today, though, had simply not been pleasant.

Fayvel did not have an extensive nor a luxurious house, but he had a lot of relatives, and he planned on finding space for all of them. His upper room would do, he said, and the Great God would make his oil and flour last just as he had for the widow...not that it hurt to be prepared. And as the relatives came, mostly men representing their families, showing up to report to the Romans and be counted, Fayvel kept Zeer busy with the flour and oil. She made more bread than she ever had before, filling the biggest bowl with dough and wrestling it with her thin arms before carrying it to the oven. While she had kept an eye on the baking, she had worked to grind the spices that kept the vast pot of soup aromatic in spite of frequent additions of water. Fayvel also had her sweep the first floor of the house after every arrival to make sure he continued to look good for the next relative.

And each one of those relatives was greeted with the same joy as the last. Fayvel remembered every name, every father's name and father's father's name, where each man had come from, and usually something that had been done in youth that was shushed and grimaced over. Perhaps not all of his knowledge was fully welcomed, even though his roof and his good humor were. Fayvel was given much leeway in his reminiscences for the sake of the smell of Zeer's soup.

As a mere servant girl, however, Zeer did not get any such leeway. As soon as one relative was stowed away, a mat set out for them and their baggage settled, another one arrived. Fayvel stood at the door, his large belly protruding beyond the frame, to greet each with a great whiskery embrace, as he simultaneously handed satchels to Zeer, and called for water and wine to be brought for the arrival. The relatives gave him "gifts" of coin in exchange for his warm hospitality, and tried not to encourage his stories of their youthful escapades.

Zeer welcomed the lessening light with all that she had left to think with. Once it was dark, very few people would try to continue to travel and this terrible day would be over. It had been so much work preparing for the onslaught of relatives, and the onslaught itself had been frantically busy, and she just needed all of it to be done. When there was finally no sound except well-fed snoring from both Fayvel's side of the house and the upper rooms, Zeer was able to stumble to her corner where her own mat and blanket were kept, and curl up within her own little space. She had hoped to be able to rest immediately, but found that she was just too tired to actually sleep. Her body ached, her mind was numb, and so she lay there staring at the firelight on the ceiling. Because she was the only one awake, though, she heard the soft voices outside first.

However much she had hoped those voices would just continue on, they did not. They paused, they talked about "the fourth house from the fountain," and "my father's brother's brother-in-law," and too soon there was a hesitant knock at the door.

Fayvel snorted. And then snored again. The wine had been good tonight.

The hesitant knock was repeated, although a bit louder this time, and Zeer began to panic about the idea of the upstairs relatives waking and needing more of anything. If they stayed asleep, they'd leave her alone. She crept out of her nest and tiptoed to Fayvel.

"*Mar*," she said, stretching out her hand like a cautious little paw and tapping his shoulder, "*Mar*, please wake up. Someone else is here now...."

Fayvel snorted again, but this time snorted himself awake. "Eh? Whaaa....you say? Who?"

"I don't know, *Mar*, someone....at the door..." and this time Fayvel also heard that hesitant knock as the person outside decided to be persistent.

Fayvel sat and scratched his extended belly and rubbed the top of his head. He slowly stood up from his bed, and stumbled to the door...more or less in a straight line. That wine tonight had actually been very good--he needed to keep buying from that woman at the market. She may be a midwife in her spare time, but when it came to wine, she certainly knew what she was talking about.

Fayvel finally got to the door and unlatched it, swinging it open to reveal a tired and worried face with a large dark shadow behind its back. "Fayvel, son of Abdiel?" asked the face. "I'm Yosef, son of Eli, brother to...."

"Hmm. Yes, brother to Eliud, my sister's husband. Hmm. I see."

"We were hoping that you would still have room for family?"

"'We,' young Yosef? There may be room for an 'I,' but there is no room for a 'we.' Who do you have with you?"

"M-my....well, my wife, Fayvel. Miryam came with me."

Zeer could feel Fayvel's scowl from clear behind him, and felt sorry for those who had to face it. She'd been in that position often enough, and she never liked it one bit. Fayvel crossed his arms and planted his feet more firmly in the doorway.

"Hmm. Yes, we heard about your wife. Very charitable of you, young Yosef. Let's see her."

Yosef gulped and turned towards the shadows at his back. He said something too soft to hear, and got no response. "Miryam?" he asked a little more loudly, and there was a soft exhale before a delayed "Is it the right house, Yosef? Is everything all right?"

"All right, young lady?" asked Fayvel, much more loudly than was necessary. "I have a full house, full of men, and now there is a...woman...turned up on my door, when I was not expecting such, and oh, the stories about you...even here, we have heard of your situation!" His words caused Yosef to turn suddenly, letting some light fall on the woman's face as she suddenly doubled forward, one hand reaching out to grab into the donkey's mane as she exhaled forcefully.

"Eh? Eh, I see....I see....the stories are all true, and here you are, and here you'll stay for a bit, and we need to find you a place right away for some privacy, of course. Well, it can't be in my house. Eh, Yosef, I'm not leaving you in the street with what you've got happening tonight, but I've a household full of men, and not a single other female about except our servant girl," he turned, squinting into the shadows to find Zeer. Zeer did not want to be seen and called to help more family. She just wanted to be left alone to rest. But Fayvel spotted her in the shadows and waved his hand at her.

"She won't be the kind of help you need, and this house is just not the place for you. And all of Beit-Lechem will be the same, every house full up and all of men. *Most* people leave their families and servants to care for things at home when taking a journey like this. The best we can do is the stable; it will at least be private, there's straw for some bedding, and who knows? That may even be more comfortable than the mats that Zeer has woven..."

It was then that Zeer realized how long it had been since she had been able to do anything more in the stable besides throw food down for their donkey. It was usually her favorite place with its sweet smells of hay and the breath of the gentle animals, but she'd been kept so busy about the house that she had not taken care of the stable like she usually did. She could only imagine the state it was in. But she accepted a lamp from Fayvel--it was the poor one that spit and only offered a feeble light--and nodded at the young couple as she edged out of the door and hesitantly showed them the way to the stable.

Miryam was tired of holding herself up, but she could feel the chill of the stone floor through her sandals, and the stones were too rough to kneel on. While she was nearly knocked over by her pains, standing was better than laying in the straw, which rustled all on its own. Miryam could only imagine how many families of rats lived out here, away from too-regular human interference. A little more of that interference might have made the stable smell a bit better, as well...when Yosef tried to help her down onto a soft pile of straw, there was a pile that was a bit too soft, and cold and damp, and now her robe smelled of it, too. She had asked him to help her right back up. It didn't matter what was happening, she would not be laying down directly on that straw. She felt the start of another tightening, and held onto a post as she sank back into a crouch, and the smells and the rustling disappeared for a minute. It was a relief when her stomach released its grip, but then it meant that the smells came back.

A different quality of rustling got her attention, while Yosef continued to unload the donkey outside so that he could get to a blanket. As Miryam raised her head, a young face poked its scared little nose around the corner. The girl was surely the servant that had led them here, but Miryam hadn't been able to see her face before. She was so small, and her features so pointed, that she almost seemed a kind of mouse herself. In a soft voice, with a bit of squeak to it, the little nervous face with the soft brown hair asked "*Domina?* What do you need?" Miryam focused her eyes, and tried to focus her mind.

"A midwife, child. Surely there is one...?"

"Yes, there is, but, *Domina*.....Sophia is Roman. Would you want her....?"

"If she is all there is, I just....please, go get her...." and the smells of the stall faded away as the grip in her stomach became her whole world again. Miryam did not hear the little one scurry away, nor did she hear Yosef's sound of triumph as he got the blanket off of the donkey and carried it into the stable.

Zeer hurried down the streets of the town, finding her way to the building where Sophia kept both her wine shop and home. Hopefully she was home this night, and Zeer would not have to go running off down more darkened streets, but could just go back to her corner and curl up again. The wine shop was shuttered, but light glowed out of the upstairs windows, and it gave Zeer hope. Her knock, however, was more hesitant than the man Yosef's was earlier that night.

There was no reply, no sound within, no flicker in that glow.

Zeer knocked again, summoning up sufficient strength and energy to make it heard. This time there was a movement in the light, and the sound of heavy footsteps stumbling closer. The door opened, and Sophia's servant, a huge, shaggy man who still wore a Gallish torque around his neck leaned against the doorframe and pushed his disheveled head towards Zeer.

"Who?" he grumbled. His Latin was as shaggy as his hair, and Zeer wondered if he'd picked up any of the local Aramaic.

"One who needs the services of the midwife. Is she here?"

"No...closed early. Some woman. Baby coming. Left wine shop early--finally quiet."

He belched, and Zeer backed away from the fumes in his breath. She wondered briefly how good the wine would be when it was sold tomorrow, and if Sophia or her customers would be the first to notice how watered down it was.

"Where? Do you know where Sophia is?"

"No...errr...end of town. By the fountain. Good fountain--Roman fountain."

Well, the Romans had only built one fountain in the city...those whose families had lived here since the Babylonian times used the wells.   It helped Zeer a little, but oh, she was tired. Did that woman in the stable really matter so very much? Could she possibly just birth on her own? Then she remembered that lone woman's face--she had such bravery and simple kindness while she had spoken with Zeer. In between her pains, it had cost her an obvious effort to gather her thoughts, and she had looked around at the poor place in which labored, still turning to speak to Zeer gently. Zeer cringed as she tried to count how many days it had been since she had tended to the stable. It was through her own neglect that the stable was smelly and dirty, but the woman laboring there never even curled a nostril. At the very least, Zeer would go to the part of town with the fountain to find this midwife and bring her to the aid of that kind woman. She only glanced once down the road in the direction of Fayvel's home, then turned and walked out of the market area.

When she finally stood by the fountain, Zeer scanned the streets that branched out from it. The houses were large here, and many were in the Roman style; forbidding fronts with well-wrought doors. The windows of the houses would all open inwardly, so there weren't many clues to help Zeer figure out which household would be in the twins of both turmoil and hope that came when a woman had a baby. As she turned about, looking for some sign of rejoicing, lamenting, or just plain activity in the dead of night, she heard a door open.

"Thank Ha Shem," she breathed, hoping to see the midwife coming out. Instead, it was a servant girl like herself, just one who seemed stronger and more assured. Zeer had a moment of panic, but if she was going to make this long night worth anything, she had to be brave.

"Please? Is the midwife here?'

The other girl turned her head quickly, her shoulders up and arms tense. "Who is there?"

Zeer stepped closer so that she could be seen more easily. "I am looking for the midwife. Is she here?"

"She is."

Zeer sighed at the lack of helpfulness. This girl was going to make her work for any information, and she had hoped to be done quickly. She tried to smile, and made an attempt at friendliness.

"I hope that there is a new child in the household, and the mother safely delivered."

The other girl eased her shoulders.

"There is. A hard birth and some blood lost, but all seems to be well for the time. They are giving thanks to Juno Lucina now, and the father has already lifted the child to claim him."

"Can the midwife leave? There is another woman...."

"She is not done with her rites. She will be soon." Zeer's own shoulders slumped; she did not like the thought of waiting in the open for the interminable Roman rites to be completed. The other girl softened further.

"Come in, offer thanks with us, tell the midwife of this other woman. It should not be long."

Zeer followed her into the small door, and down the dim walkway to a small flight of stairs at the back of the house. She knew she could not make an offering to any Roman god, but she was so far into this errand that it must be completed. Before she could puzzle out how to work through this situation, she was led into a well-lit and well-warmed room, full of people. A man in a hastily-fastened toga was holding a squawking pile of blankets, an exhausted woman lay resting on a real bed, not just a straw mat like Zeer had prepared for guests, and two women were beginning to snuff out a dish of burning incense, placed before one of the thousands of different *Lares* that the Romans chose from for their household deities. There was a dark stain on the floor close to a bowl that contained a wet mass--the afterbirth, Zeer guessed. She carefully avoided that stain as she approached the two women.

"Please...Sophia? There is a woman...."

The older of the two in front of the bowl of incense turned, her hands in her hair as she re-bound it. "Yes? Another servant? You are late for the offering to Juno Lucina...."

"No, Sophia, not one of mine..." rumbled the pleased new *Pater.*

"There is a woman. She is a traveler, and in labor, and in my master's stable, and she is alone! Please. Sophia, will you come to her?"

"Well, it's a busy night. But Juno Lucina will always accept more offerings. Speaking of which, Patricius....?"

The new father rumbled happily again. "Of course, Sophia. Good work done tonight. An offering to you and your Juno Lucina is well deserved." And bright coins clinked into a pouch that the midwife held out. Zeer thought of the small donkey that this couple had arrived on, the few bags, the strong but humble cloth they were clothed in, and wondered how much of an offering they would be able to give. Even then, offerings would only be to Sophia, not her idol. While Zeer considered these possibilities, Sophia continued to tuck things into a basket and a large satchel. That other servant girl entered with a tray of cups of wine, and after handing one to the new mother, Sophia drank hers in three great gulps. She grinned at the Roman when she was done. "Patricius, next time you buy wine, come to my shop. This is good, but I can get you better."

Patricius gave a short laugh. "Woman, when you stop buying Gallish slaves to watch over your wine, I'll buy from you exclusively. I've smelt the wine on your man's breath, and what I bought that day was not as pure as it should have been. I believe that when you're away, he helps himself quite freely, but makes sure that the levels in the jars are the same. Perhaps check the levels of your water jars when you get back to your shop, hmmm?"

Sophia tilted her head to the side and put one hand on a hip. The look on her face was exactly the same that Fayvel turned to Zeer when he was displeased, and Zeer found herself edging towards the door. She wasn't even the object of Sophia's anger, and she still wanted to get farther away from it. After glaring at Patricius for a moment, Sophia finally answered him. "I will be sure to check those jars. But you be sure to come by tomorrow, and I promise you will purchase better wine than you served me tonight. I will see you then." Patricius let out another short laugh, and Sophia turned to look for Zeer. "Where…? Ah. Child, stop lurking in corners. Show me where this next mother is laboring." With Sophia following closely, Zeer crept out of the room, down the stairs, and began her next journey back to the stable.

It had been a frustrating walk back to the stable. Zeer had wanted to hurry along silently, but Sophia had to haul a considerably greater girth, and she didn't seem capable of being silent. She was pleased at how the Roman woman's birth had just gone, and ambled happily as she told Zeer about it. "For many hours, it seemed this baby would never come, but the grandmother had made sure to have a ladder handy. Oh, we shook her on that for so long...it's important to tie their feet well with scarves when you do so, or they just fall off and that doesn't help one get the baby. When her pains were closer together, we helped her down and made her climb stairs. Oh, she didn't like that, no, not at all but old Sophia knows how to keep a mother moving!" Zeer wished that Sophia knew how to get herself moving a little more, and reached out to help carry the midwife's bag. Perhaps if Sophia weren't so burdened, she could walk faster. The motion startled Sophia.

"What? Oh, be careful with that, child. Not only are my tools in there, but the statue of Juno Lucina. We don't want her jostled and offended before asking her assistance for another woman! No, we don't want that at all...." Zeer, even though now shouldering a significant burden, simply started to walk more quickly. She wished she could outpace Sophia's words, but she was needed to lead Sophia carefully. There were several inns and each had their own stables, and Sophia wouldn't be familiar with this part of the city. The midwife was soon huffing as she tried to keep up with the girl who carried her birthing tools.

"Child, slow up….it does not do any good to arrive at a birth in a hurry. Babies don't hurry, they come at their own time. How much farther do we need to go? Wait...isn't she in the inn? What is back here?"

Zeer glanced back. "There was no room, *Domina*. Only the stable." She had spoken so quietly that Sophia had needed to be quiet herself in order to hear, and as they approached, they were both able to hear a soft moan. That moan briefly became a grunt before softening again, and then trailing into silence. Zeer remembered the stain on the floor of the Roman house, and shied back from entering the stable. Sophia, however, quickened her pace.

"By the sound of it, this might not be a long labor. After that last one, a quick birth would be a kindness--both to me and the mother. Girl, I will need water--the warmer the better, but quickly is best. Also, cloth. But it must be clean. Hurry, girl...." and the two separated, one filled with relief as she fled the uncertainty of birth, one ready to work and be at her best and sharpest.

As Sophia entered the dim stable, she had to squint to be able to tell where this laboring mother was. She followed the sound of shaky breathing into the corner and found the mother laying on a thick blanket in the straw. She knelt down and stroked the woman's hair. "Well, *dominula,* you sound nearly ready to have your baby. I am here, and I can perform the rites for Juno Lucina, but there may not be time. However, at the least I can bring her out so that she may witness your birth. And I will loosen my girdle and hope it brings you a loose and easy birth."

There was a deep sound of confusion from the side of the stable closer to the door, and Sophia turned her head to see a figure standing close by. She didn't have time to ask him anything before the young mother began another soft moan and reached out. Sophia held her hand while she listened to the moan once again become a bit of a grunt before softening back down. "Well, no, there is not time to even get Juno out. Let us see how close your baby is, and I will help you get the little one out. We'll discuss rites and offerings afterward...."

While Sophia helped the young mother re-position herself, she looked closely at her clothes and the blanket that had been under her. It was all well-made but quite humble, meant to be more sturdy than beautiful. A quick birth would be just as well, since these travelers didn't look wealthy enough to pay for her full services. She would only be needed to help this woman get her baby out--not to make the labor itself go well.

When Zeer re-appeared, sidling carefully around the doorway with a bucket of tepid water and a length of cloth under her arm, Sophia looked up with a bewildered and baffled face. The midwife was crouching down in front of the laboring woman, who was now laying back on the thick blanket that covered the straw. The husband was still there, off to the side, unsure of himself. If Sophia had not been so astonished at something, she would certainly have ordered him off by now--birth was no place for men. Zeer eyed him sideways as she crept around the other edge of the stable. This birth was certainly unlike the others she'd heard of. When were men ever around? And what could knock the words out of a midwife--this one in particular?

Sophia was looking hard at the young mother. "I do not understand. Your baby is nearly here....but how did there come to be a baby? There is something there that I should not have felt....who *are* you?"

"I am only a maidservant of God. This baby...." and Miryam curled around her belly, her words starting to come just in grunts. "...this baby...is...born of God..."

That was not reassuring to Sophia. "Which god? Even when Jupiter fathers his many children, it is in a natural way...this is new. I cannot perform the correct rites if I do not know which god to offer them *to!*"

At this, the quiet man in the corner finally spoke. "It is the Almighty God, Ha Shem, the God of Avraham, Yitzchak, and Ya`akov, who has brought this baby into being. And now he must come, and come well. Are you able, midwife?"

Sophia pulled herself together with visible surprise. "A Hebrew? And here I am, able to petition Juno but helping a Hebrew baby be born...and surely one who was conceived in a much more powerful manner than any other baby.

Hebrew, your God must be very great. And yes, I am able to help. But you will have to make your own offerings."

Miryam gave a louder cry, reaching out and clinging to whatever she could find. Zeer had crept close and instinctively caught one of the woman's hands, surprised by the strength with which Miryam held on. As the mother pulled, Zeer began to lose her balance, and Sophia relaxed back into her knowledge and habits. "Lean back, child, she needs your weight to help her. Lady...curl around this baby, let me bend your knees. You...the father..or, no? Husband? Not yet, at least not fully....argh, what *is* your name?"

"Yosef."

"And her name?"

"Miryam."

"Good. Miryam, curl around this child, brace your foot here against me, your Yosef will hold the other..."

And into the dark of the stable, with the flicker of just the one poor lamp, a baby emerged from an impossible mother into the hands of a silenced Roman midwife. Sophia was aghast at the entire event and breathed out her amazement of the workings of this Hebrew God before becoming brisk again.

"Quickly, child, the smaller of the cloths. Help me rub him down so that he does not become chilled--ah, he is well formed. No need to worry, he breathes well and on his own..." Sophia was talkative and capable again, rubbing and lifting and examining, telling the new mother all she saw.

"Do not lift him yet, Miryam. We must not pull the afterbirth, but let it come gently on its own. But be assured, your son is well and strong. He does not cry, but he is well. In fact, I have never seen a child newly born who looked so content. He actually looks joyful!" Miryam smiled and reached down to stroke her son's head. She swallowed painfully and Zeer wondered if she'd hurt her throat with all that grunting. There wasn't anything in the stable to drink water from, so Zeer cupped her hand and lifted water from the bucket to Miryam. Miryam smiled at her, drank, and turned to Sophia.

"That last bit of time on the donkey was terrible, and then everything seemed so fast...is it often that babies come so quickly?"

"A donkey? Gods be praised--or is it? Perhaps just the one God...I've never seen the likes of this...at any rate, that jostling on the donkey is probably what sped it all up. No need to tie you to a ladder and shake *you*! Not that Soranus likes that practice, anyhow, and I usually agree with his writings, although he is a man." Sophia continued to tend to the baby and the mother, using Zeer's bucket of water now to rinse and wring cloths out. She had tied the cord and offered the quiet father a knife with which to separate the baby from his mother, and was now preparing to get the little one settled on his mother's chest when they heard approaching footsteps. The footsteps were hurried, and varied...it was several people who were coming quickly and loudly to the stable. Sophia once again became brisk and efficient.

"No privacy in this stable! Quickly, a blanket over the mother...Miryam, you will need to set your baby down for a moment, let us get you covered before someone pokes their head in here, He's well wrapped, just next to you..."

"No--" protested Miryam. "Don't set him on the straw! Sophia....it...rustles!"

Sohpia looked at her blankly for a moment as she took this in. "True, it would. I don't usually need to consider rustling straw." One corner of her mouth twitched up into a bit of a smile. "But then, you weren't either, were you? Well, Yosef, do you have a place to hold the baby that does not rustle?"

Yosef had been moving to the entry of the stable, to either block or wave on as needed, and he frowned briefly. "What about the manger? That should be fresher straw..."

"Yes, absolutely. Miryam, I'll set him there, still close, but pull that blanket up a bit farther, *dominula*...."

Just as the baby was settled in the manger, the commotion became visible as well as audible. The glow of a lantern--one much better than what Fayvel had sent--grew on the wall of the stable. With the brighter light, the voices also changed from indiscernible mutterings to actual words.

"Would this stable have a manger, do you think? Is it the right type?

"Looks big enough..."

"Someone's in here, there's a light."

A man's shaggy head, nearly as wooly as the sheep in nearby fields, appeared around the side of the doorway. His eyes looked past Yosef and swept around the little building, pausing first on the blanket-covered woman, and then opening wide at the sight of the little swaddled bundle in the manger.

"Here! It's here! I found the baby--come here!"

More shaggy heads, with the short, loose robes of shepherds, appeared. There could only have been four or five of them, but in that small stable already filled with people, it seemed like a crowd. Crowds were usually noisy, though, and these newcomers became still and hushed as soon as they pressed in around the manger. They stared in a shocked silence at the baby lying there.

"It's real."

"We really saw them; they really said everything."

"What does this mean? How do we know what to do?"

Miryam started to become alarmed at this odd behavior. She struggled to sit up more and wave them back from her baby. Sophia saw this and stepped in between the shepherds and the manger.

"What are you talking about, and why on earth are you walking right in? This woman has just brought out her child, there is a need for privacy! Back away, you--all of you!"

A few men glanced down and Miryam, finally registering that a newly born babe meant a newly delivered woman. Yosef was elbowing his way through the unkempt group to stand by Sophia, guarding his wife and child. Zeer remained by Miryam, heaping the straw behind her back to support her in sitting up at least a little. She had always liked the shepherds, with their easy, kind manners. They were humble men, who would not normally press in where they weren't wanted. The shepherds shifted as a group, moving back slightly. "Our apologies, *Domina*....we are confused, ourselves. Such things as we've seen--it makes no sense. But, *Domina*, there...there were angels."

Miryam and Yosef exchanged a glance. They seemed to know what it was to be visited by angels.

Sophia did not have any such experience, and had no patience for talk that surely was only dreams or the effect of too-strong wine. "Out. If that's all you have for an excuse..."

"No, *Domina*, listen. The angels were specific...a babe newborn, well-wrapped, but in a manger. It made no sense. Why would anyone set a baby in a manger? But we see now. And the angels...like nothing any of us have seen or heard. Such glory! And those beings, full of glory themselves, giving glory to God. I've always gone to the Temple for the Feast, but I had no idea of how great the Almighty is. I never thought of anything so glorious as these angels, and they were singing the praises of God! They told us about this baby--they said that his birth was news of great joy. How great is a baby when his birth gives such joy to such beings? There are no words. But they told us how to find him--we've been searching stables in Beit-Lechem for an hour. And here he is, wrapped up and laying in a manger. It is so strange, and so wonderful. Angels, *Domina*. Angels like you've never heard, and this is why they came. What do we do?"

Sophia was quiet for a moment as she tried to make sense of this. "I do not know what your God would have you do. This baby has been born in the strangest way-- surely divine, but not like any god I've ever heard of. But, no matter how this baby came to be, he is still a baby and he needs his mother. You need to leave. You've seen him, you've told about your angels, it's time for you to go." She didn't give them a chance to think about it as she started to physically push them towards the stable door. Zeer realized that she had been holding her breath the whole time, full of conflicting emotions. She held both awe and joy over the story of glorious angels with worry for Miryam and a bit of fear of this herd of men crowding about. As they left, she started to breathe again, and once again assisted with arranging blankets.

Sophia sat and gazed at the puny flame of the meager lamp. Without looking away, she spoke to Zeer. "Child, bring the baby to his mother, he needs to nurse. He's still a baby, no matter if he's born of a maid and heralded by angels. Still a baby...whoever he may be, and whatever his destiny."

Zeer crept out from behind Miryam, and eased her hands under the baby. This was Zeer's first good look at him, and she found herself smiling freely in response to the happy little expression on his face. She'd felt afraid of lifting a baby at first, but looking at him eased her fears. And then, Sophia had him so well wrapped that he felt like a solid bundle. She carried him back to his mother.

Miryam was silent as she received her son back into her arms. She held him close, breathing in the scent of his head, looking into his eyes. He was so calm and filled with joy. He was still a baby, but his eyes held so much more. And the angels rejoiced at his birth.

RETURN

Achim did not like waking up. Sleeping meant
forgetfulness. It was only in sleep that he was able to set
aside his cares and his shame and his attempts at self-
protection. So many others had stumbled off to their mats,
set themselves down with the setting of the sun, and not
woken; this was the shared and unspoken hope for every
member of the camp. Perhaps this was the night where they
would sleep and not have to see the sun rise again.

It was with this thought that Achim dragged his stumps
of feet each night toward his corner of the camp of the
Dead Ones--he remembered that there had once been a boy
who could run!--and used the great stones on either side of
his mat to help him lower himself down. Those memories
of the boy he had once been always came unbidden, and
they always caused fresh pain. When he had ceased to be

that boy, he had lost so much, and the memories made everything about his existence now even worse.

He listened to the muttering of the other Dead Ones, as they worshiped and petitioned the many gods who had foothold in the land. He could always tell who had recently been cast out of their homes and found their way here...they prayed for healing and for the loved ones that they'd left. When life as a leper had long become their regular existence, they only prayed for life to end. Achim had been in the camp long enough that those memories of the boy who had once lived were usually distant, and he did not add to the whisperings that swirled about him. Every night his heart made the same plea: "HaShem, you have already killed me. Please do not make me live another day." And each morning as awareness grew with the light, his despair increased. He did not want to be awake again. He did not want to smell the infection in his own skin or see the rats scurry away with his movement or hear the rattles and moans of those who were more awake and more mobile as they began their cries for the day. "Unclean….unclean….." they croaked by the roadside, both a warning and a plea for help.

"HaShem, I am already in Sheol. Could death be worse? Why must you punish me by forcing me to still breathe?"

As long as he was breathing, however, he must live. He remembered that there had once been a boy who felt that breathing deeply was a joy, and with anger at the memory he tried to stop his own breath. He choked all air out and attempted to close his own throat by sheer will and force of his anger. However, his own body rebelled against him once more, and air rushed into his lungs. With all the things that no longer worked, why couldn't his lungs have become diseased and failed him first? But the stubborn things insisted on continuing to pull air into his body and sustain him, just as his stomach still managed to create pain if he did not eat. So he pulled himself up, reaching for his sticks to help himself balance on what was left of his feet. Day after day, he would join the others by the roadside, keeping his face covered as he called out and sat with conflicted hope for bits of bread to keep his body alive.

The custom amongst the Dead Ones was to try to guess the religious beliefs of the passers-by, and appeal to the god they most likely worshiped. If it was a Centurion, they called to Mars to give him success in battle. If there was the nose of a Persian, the Dead Ones cried out in the name of Ahura Mazda. If there was the phylactery of a Jew, they cried to the One who had made the lions go away...acknowledging that it was the Hebrew God who had shown himself more powerful than the others, generations and generations ago. Achim remembered that there had once been a boy who sat warm by a fire and listened to the stories. Being dead now meant that he rarely felt cold, but he also never felt truly warm. And nobody told the stories anymore.

Of course, even the Dead Ones still knew those stories...they were as much a part of the land as the stones. For more than twenty generations, the land remembered the lions that had come, and the people reminded each other of that terrible time. Every god that every family had ever worshiped had been petitioned, but none of them were strong enough or pleased enough to hold back the lions, and every home knew loss. Messengers had been sent to the king in Assyria--if he were going to conquer the people and exact tribute from them, could they not get assistance? The king had made his own consultations, and finally brought Hebrew priests into the land. Before the Assyrians had conquered them and moved people around, Samaria had been a part of Israel...but the Israelite God was the last one to be honored again after their exile. It was only when the priests set up a holy place in Bethel where HaShem could be worshiped that the lions finally went away. The power of the Hebrew God was strong enough to allow safety in the land. In spite of that safety, though, the people had learned to fear the things that could happen if worship were insufficient. They were afraid of taking any risks. Perhaps the Hebrew God had only been the final bit of strength, and perhaps he had worked in accord with the other gods in the land. It was vital then that they would all get their due...as long as the lions stayed away.

Achim wondered if the lions could possibly be as great a threat as the rats--if he'd been attacked by a lion, his end would have been far quicker. With the rats, he only discovered missing bits here and there. And Achim never was sure who to turn his worship towards, but he usually prayed to the God of the Hebrews. His family had once been Israelite before everything got muddled by the Assyrians, and they had been careful to keep the traditions of Israel as best as they could. Either their one God was strong enough on his own to banish the lions, and thus strong enough to let Achim finally rest, or none of the gods were. Either way, keeping track of the offerings and prayers and names of every possible deity was exhausting. And it was obvious that the interminable prayers of his fellow Dead weren't helping them anyways.

As long as HaShem decided to stay silent and ignore his prayers, though, and as long as his stubborn body held on to life, he had to assist it. Besides, sitting on his mat all day feeling angry had been a terrible idea. Those days were the longest and hardest to get through--he remembered that there had once been a boy who felt that the days were too short!--and he did not want to have to live through such days anymore. Begging by the side of the road at least offered diversions and things to think about as the living people moved past. After the game of guessing at their favorite idols, there were all the other aspects of life to wonder at...did that man have a family? Was there a wife at his house, ready to greet him when he got home? Did the young man have a good relationship with his father, or were they ever opposed to each other, as fathers and sons have often found themselves to be since the beginning? Did the group of women leaving town feel successful in their sales of bread or vegetables or whatever cloth they had woven? Achim remembered that there had once been a boy who followed his father to the market….and ah, that boy had died when he had not felt the coal from the hearth under his foot, and the spots were discovered. The earth pulled his heart downward as his eyes tried again to form tears to grieve the loss of that boy. But even his eyes betrayed him, and he was unable to shed a single tear.

So he adjusted his wrappings and heaved himself up, finding his sticks to keep his balance on his withered feet. Slowly he made his way to the roadside, only stumbling twice today, and took up a place amongst the other Dead. He maintained some distance from the others, and they spread out far along the road. They all still felt the abhorrence of getting too close to one struck down with leprosy, even though they were all similarly struck. Perhaps they all remembered the boys who once had been, and those boys had been well taught of the abomination of this disease. They may have that abomination dwelling in their own flesh now, but the memory of revulsion toward this disease was strong, even from one leper to another. The camp of the Dead Ones was a miserable place, and at the roadside they carried their lonely misery with them.

Achim did not even know the names of those who stood closest to him. He knew them by the faded colors of their garments, one who had been loved enough as a boy that his robe had stripes woven into it, another who had lost more of his face and sight than most, and kept all but one clouding eye fully veiled. He knew the shape of their hands under the wrappings of rags--it was rare for a Dead One to keep his hands unwrapped. Fingers were easy targets for the rats. He also knew them by the sound of their voices, some with harsh, guttural croaks and some still having the ability to call out clearly. There was one leper who had been at the camp the longest, and he rarely spoke.

When he did, his speech was nearly indiscernible, so slurred and slow that the others were horrified at the devastation they could only guess at. He kept himself closely wrapped so that none of them could actually see what had happened to his face, and his calls along the road were little more than guttural grunts. Achim himself was able to call clearly, although his voice was no longer perfectly smooth. He did not try too hard to disguise this damage to his voice, as he knew that calling out with that brokenness made him an object of greater pity. Often, he would be the recipient of more bread than the others, and he would leave some of it on the stones in the middle of their camp. He never knew who came and took any of it, but it always disappeared too quickly and too completely for it to have been the rats.

After tottering and stumbling his way to his normal spot, he lowered himself into the dust. It was no longer possible for him to stand through the days at the side of the road. His balance was not good after his feet had become diseased, and his hands were too dead for him to trust how well he was gripping his sticks. At least he could not feel the discomfort from kneeling on the hard road. If he must beg, he could crouch there all day without his body stopping him. And if the blood in his legs turned purple from the lack of movement, his wrappings kept the discoloration out of sight. He knew of others whose feet and legs had grown blackened and then stank of infection...and it had hastened their death. Achim almost welcomed the thought. So he settled himself down, and he begged, calling out with a harsh voice and clear speech, asking for those who were alive to be kind to those who were dead.

Today was more promising from the start. It was the day of preparation for the Hebrew Sabbath, so the market was busier than normal as people bought and sold a little extra to carry them over two days. The road had groups coming up from the country, hastening to get a good spot in town for their tables. The Dead Ones were familiar with some, either by their faces or their donkeys, and knew that several of them would be generous. The donkey with the black forelock came as usual, and the man leading it slowed as he approached the part of the road lined with filthy rags. He kept his head turned away, avoiding even eye contact, but set the large leaf he had been using as a fan into the dust, and pulled four small loaves of bread out of the donkey's bags. He piled the bread on the leaf, added a small handful of olives, and hurried away. Once he was a safe distance from the disease, he slowed down to a normal pace. That was the signal for the Dead Ones to rush at the small pile of food, trying not to touch each other but also desperate to grasp at some of the fresh bread before the others. Achim wasn't quick enough today with his stumps and his sticks, and he turned back cursing both his clumsiness and his hunger. And yet, if he starved, death would come more quickly, what did it matter if it hurt?

Some kind women, as they walked to market, saw the group of rags along the side of the road and paused. One of the women focused particularly on one of the newcomers, a leper who still stood upright and wore actual clothes instead of frayed rags. While his face was well covered, she obviously recognized him and stood quiet with tears falling from her cheeks, raising puffs of dust from the ground where they dropped. After a long moment where silence and grief flowed freely between the two of them, she reached into a pouch at her waist and pulled out four eggs, setting them by the marks her tears had made at her feet. She held her hand over her heart as her breath came in short gasps, then turned her back on the row of lepers and walked on with stumbling steps. The Dead One who had held her eyes for such a long time watched her leave, then slowly moved toward the group of eggs on the road. His fingers were clumsy through their wrappings, so he used a fold of cloth to cradle the eggs. As he crossed back to the side that the lepers inhabited, he paused to see the others watching him carefully. He turned to the side and placed one egg an arm's reach in front of Achim. It was not close enough for them to worry about touching each other, but his gift was obvious. He moved to place another egg also within arm's reach of another leper, and then curled his own arm to hold the remaining two eggs close to his heart. Achim enjoyed his egg very much; it was still warm from having been roasted by some hearth, and carried the memory of warm bread and comfortable sounds with it. He never saw if his fellow leper ever actually ate those eggs himself, or if he just continued to sit through the day holding that precious gift.

After the heat of mid-day, when the glaring sun had started to draw close to the horizon and a fresh breath of a breeze flowed along the road, the Dead Ones saw a larger group come into view. Many groups had come from town like this one, done with the day's work of trading or visiting family, going back to their homes and fields in the country. However, this group was larger than most of the others. Ten or fifteen men walked as a cluster, one in the middle smiling and talking as he went. The others were obviously focused on him, asking him questions and nodding occasionally at one another. At their approach, the chorus of croaks and pleas began again. There was no obvious indication of which god to appeal to, so they focused their calls on the one man who seemed to be the center of attention. "Please, master, have pity!" "Have pity, lord, help us!" "Master, can you spare any aid?" "Mercy, master, mercy!" The cries went on as wrapped hands extended in appeal.

The man in the center of the group stopped and looked at the pitiful bundles of rags stretched along the side of the road. Instead of keeping his face turned away, he looked at each of the Dead in turn, with kindness in his eyes. He actually started to smile at them, as if there were anything to smile about. Without turning away from their disease, but also without moving to give any of them food, he quietly told them "Go. Show yourselves to the priests." After that he again looked at each one in turn, gently nodded his head, and began to walk down the road once more. His followers began to move with him, but they shifted their positions to keep him between themselves and the lepers, casting worried glances back at the ragged group as they left. The one who was closest to their leader was heard to ask "But

Master, if they're here, they've already shown themselves to the priests. How can…."

His question echoed the thoughts of the group by the road. The man who still held those two eggs close in the crook of his arm spoke out loud. "Could the priest have been wrong? Could I be clean somehow? If I could return home…" The other Dead Ones knew better. The disease had ravaged their bodies long enough, and that damage had been significant enough, that they had no doubts of what they were. Still, when the man with the eggs turned and began to walk down the road, their faces turned with him and a few feet shuffled. The leper closest to Achim moved a few halting steps, then stopped and turned back towards his former place along the edge. "What is the use?" Achim heard him mutter before he paused, still hesitating in the middle of the road. He gazed after the lepers who were already moving before also asking, "But then, why not? I have nowhere else to go…." He turned again and began his stumbling steps once more, and two more lepers were drawn out of their huddled postures after him. They became a slow band of their own, dragging away from that one quiet man within his group of whole-bodied men. But their doubts were as tangible as the cloud of dust that was kicked up by their shumbling movements.

"Which priest are we supposed to go see? There are so many…"

"He said priests…perhaps all of them."

Many well-wrapped heads nodded. That made sense.

"It took all the gods to get rid of the lions, perhaps if we go visit all the temples and all the priests, they will all work together to get rid of this disease."

The man with the eggs shook his head. "No. It took HaShem, the God of the Hebrews, to get rid of the lions."

The one who rarely spoke tried now, and they realized again the terror of what awaited them, as his speech was slurred almost beyond comprehension. None of them had seen his face, so they did not know exactly how his mouth or tongue had been ravaged, but they could guess as he struggled to communicate. "err-ha...a...ps...He-vrew Go..o...d 'us jus...the las...st."

"So, should we see his priest first, or last, then?"

"First." Achim was surprised at his own clarity and certainty. "Whether he was the final bit of strength, or the only one with real strength, he should be honored first."

"Yes, good," was the croaking beside him. "And then we will visit all the others in turn, and make sure they all get their due. If healing is possible, we must make sure that we do everything that we can." None of them questioned that quiet, kind man who had given them this directive; trust and action flowed behind him, sweeping away their doubts as naturally as dry dust was carried away by the wind.

The Dead Ones were just motes of the same dust, dry bones creaking along the dry road, swept away in the wake of that trust that continued to flow, and they never knew quite when it happened. Sometime after they had started towards the town, an unfamiliar voice asked "The Temple for the Hebrew God...it's not far, is it? I'm actually hungry, and I hope that some kind soul there will be generous with a bit of bread." The group looked at the speaker in silence. Their consternation made him stop and extend his hands in apology. "I know our errand is more important than a bit of bread, but some bread would help us along in the journey, also…." his voice trailed off in the wind as he himself realized what he had done. He, who had kept himself so well wrapped that only his eye showed, and who never spoke because of the tremendous effort it took to work around missing lips, had spoken easily and clearly. Even the shape of his extended hands under his rags looked different. As he used one hand to touch the other, and then feel for his face under the diseased cloth, the others could hear him gasp. "I can feel them...I can feel…" came clearly to their ears, although he barely breathed the words.

Achim stood rooted to the ground as he watched the Dead One in the middle of their group hold himself with life and wonder. Slowly, Achim became aware of the feeling of the earth under his feet; it was solid and hard and there were little pebbles digging into the heel of his foot. He shifted his feet to find a more comfortable stance, and clenched his hands in pain as he ended up with an even sharper rock digging into a sensitive spot.

And then he stared at his hand. He could not see through his own wrappings, but he could feel each finger clenching, each fingernail pressing into his palm. Out of the corner of his eye he saw another Dead One snatching his rags away from his own face, reaching with unwrapped hands to feel the ears and nose, the smooth skin covering his cheekbones. Achim turned his face away and closed his eyes as he pulled the rags away from one hand, holding his arm out straight. He almost couldn't muster up the courage to blink his eyes open, until he heard two shouts from two different sides. There was so much excitement crackling in the air around him that his eyes opened in surprise, and he glanced quickly at his outstretched hand.

Fingers.

All five fingers, and he could wave them in the wind. Fingernails, knuckles, even some hair on the back of his hand like he remembered. He stopped holding his breath but let air rush into his lungs with joy, just the way that boy he remembered had used to breathe. His hands tried to obey his commands as he rapidly and clumsily pushed his rags farther up, revealing forearms that were smooth and brown and strong again. All along the road, wrappings were being unwound and rags were cast off into the dust. Ten men stood in the sun, feeling the breeze on their faces, smelling the fields around them, stomping on the road for the sheer joy of feeling it under their feet.

With their faces unveiled, they looked at each other as they all grew quiet. Without the rags to identify them, they had no way of knowing who they each were.   Achim felt his eyebrows raise high up on his forehead as he remembered that boy again, and the joy that boy had felt when meeting other boys at the market. He turned to the man closest to him, extending an arm in greeting.

"I am Achim, son of Abdiel."

The man extended his own hand and grasped Achim's forearm. "And I am Shem, son of Lemuel."

Another man approached Achim, his own arm extended in greeting.   The other arm stayed curled to shelter two eggs. "Achim, son of Abdiel, I am Mendel, and I am glad to both see your face, and show mine." Achim looked at the man's face in wonder, appreciating the kindness in his eyes. He had already known Mendel was kind, it was a gift now to know his name and see that quality so clearly in his face.

"Thank you for the egg."

Mendel continued to stand clasping Achim's arm as he looked down. His eyes filled with tears which dropped and left their own marks in the dust. "She is the most wonderful of women, and my only prayer was to live my life by her side….but not if it means she becomes cursed. If the priest declares me clean, I will get to return to her."

"That would be a good thing."

"A great thing. A very great thing!" He shouted and wept and finally released Achim's arm.

There was weeping and shouting and laughing all around the road as the men who had existed side by side for so many never-ending days continued to finally meet. The touch of each hand brought greater and greater wonder, and as they began to embrace each other, and slap each other on the back, the group pulled into a closer circle than they had ever done before. After the initial celebration and exchange of the names of the boys they had once been, who now could be living men, they grew quiet.

"It is a great miracle."

"Greater than any at the famed Pool of Siloam."

"Greater than the healing of Naaman--we have not washed in any river."

"We have done nothing--not even show ourselves to the priest! And yet, this is a mighty healing."

"We still must show ourselves, though, so we can return to our families."

"...my wife."

"My home...I will get to see my home again!"

"So, the priests--we must continue our journey. They need to declare us clean, healed, so that we can be with our families again."

The men who were now alive all turned to the one named Mendel. He was right, and at such a great miracle, they must not jeopardize it with a misstep. "We must do this correctly." Shem spoke with conviction. The joy of being made whole and feeling alive again was a precious joy, and there was fear amongst many of them that it may not last. They had already lost their lives once, what must they do to prevent the gods from striking them again?

"What god do you think that man served?"

"Did anyone see anything that would tell us?"

Shem, who had only had one clouded eye with which to see, spoke up. "He wore the tassels of the Hebrews. He may not have had the phylactery of the Pharisees, but he was Hebrew."

The group stood silent for a time. "Again, the Hebrew God is greatest. A servant of his merely speaks a word, and ten men are restored…"

"We must go to the Hebrew priest."

The men nodded and agreed, and once more turned their faces down the road in the direction of the Hebrew temple.   Shem pulled back a bit. "Do we bring an offering?"

This caused a pause and a bit of consternation. Eventually, Mendel spoke again. "That man only said to go show ourselves, not to bring a sacrifice. We will go, we will show our restored flesh to the priests, they can declare us clean and then let us know what offering to give. We must not neglect any step. We cannot jeopardize our healing."

Achim had been lagging at the tail end of the group as these deliberations continued. When Mendel spoke of an offering of thanks, his heart leaped in his chest. What if that were all that was needed? His healing felt complete, his body was whole again, and he was filled with the glory of joy and gratitude. As the others continued to discuss how to carefully protect their healing, Achim just felt grateful. He knew what some of the rituals were in those various temples--rituals that were meant to guard against such sickness. He knew some of the messy, heartrending things that the other gods demanded for the hope of their favor. But that one man on the road...he had done nothing, required nothing, simply walked past them with a smile and the calm instruction of showing themselves to the priests. The Dead-Who-Were-Now-Alive wanted so much to make sure that any god who had been a part of their healing got their due, but how could any of the gods be more powerful than a quiet, smiling man who could heal ten without even turning aside? Unlike any priest in any temple, he had barely paused--there had been no rites, no great prayer, no expensive sacrifice. He had given them just a few words before walking on. But the priests who served those other gods...they were only servants, and surely had less power than the idols they bowed before. If the idol itself had less power than that one man, then the servant of the idol would be even more weak in comparison.

Achim could not think of anywhere else he wanted to go to offer thanks and show himself healed besides that one man who seemed to have a kind of actual power. He was already lagging behind the rest of the group, and he listened to their debates and considerations about what they ought to do. They were still carefully discussing how to make sure that every potential was covered, and to not miss an obligation that might jeopardize their healing. But Achim turned, and set his face toward the country, in the direction that the man and his followers had walked. His first few steps away from the rest of the Healed Ones were halting-- for so long, he had lived amongst those piles of rags and disease, and he was unsure of his own movements as a solitary man. But slowly, each step became more firm as he remembered the way that the boy's feet used to meet to the earth, and the way he used to balance easily on his own legs. Suddenly, a fresh burst of wind caused the setting sun to come warm and golden out of a covering of cloud, and he remembered the boy who could run so joyfully that he felt like he was flying, free as a bird. There were finches wheeling over his head, and as he looked up, he remembered the way that boy used to spread his arms like the finches and try to mimic their ecstatic movements. Achim found himself running and leaping, his arms in the air catching at the breeze, once again a boy who was filled with the simple joy of being alive on the earth.

He was still flying and twirling and swooping with the birds when he came up to the group of men. Several of them turned puzzled faces toward him as they became aware of the irregular thumps of his footsteps. A few more recognized the rags that still clung to his body, and drew back as he continued to approach. He was used to the crinkled nostrils and pulling tight of robes. Achim's long habit had been to stop far back from all other men, and his hand instinctively lifted to cover his upper lip with some fold of cloth. However, he had shed most of his looser rags, and it was the clean, warm skin of his very own fingers that met his own face, giving him the courage to stand free and uncovered in the sun, as he and the other men looked at each other.

The leader of the group had stopped, and Achim could see his hair waving in the sun as he kept his face turned toward the man he had been conversing with. That man, however, had stopped talking and had fixed his gaze on the newcomer in leper's clothes. By now, Achim had drawn nearly close enough to breathe on the outskirts of their group.

As the leader turned to follow the attention of his companions, he still had that warm smile. There was welcome and kindness in his eyes, and he did not shrink back. He remained still and looked Achim directly in his eyes while the other men shifted and rearranged themselves.

They did pull back from Achim, but they also glanced at their leader and saw that he was not disturbed. Eventually, they formed themselves into two curved arms reaching out from the still man in the middle, and Achim took hesitant steps into the center of the circling group.

It was a joy to have control of his balance and muscles and joints, and he lowered first one knee to the ground and then the other. He could feel the roughness of earth and dust under him, and he rejoiced in every sensation. But he did not know what to say. He bent his head and pressed his fingertips to his forehead, feeling the intact skin all up to his hairline. It was all such a wonder, and in that wonder he looked up at the waiting man in front of him. He turned his palms up to receive the warmth of the sun and his fingers stretched out in the very joy of having fingers.

"Master," he said, "What can I do except seek your face and give you thanks? None of the idols have the power that you have shown. I will go to any priest you ask, but I had to come here first. I have never heard of such a healing, and I know that this came from you and not from any other. Master, I give you my thanks. I will give anything else you ask--any service, any offering...not that I have much to offer beyond my rags!"

Achim continued to kneel in the dust--he who had been a mote of dust himself, but now felt living flesh wrapping around his bones. The man in front of him reached out and clasped one of his extended hands to a chorus of sharp inhales from the group nearly encircling them. Achim was pulled to his feet, but the man did not let go. His hand was warm and strong and his grip was sure and unshrinking. And in all of it, he never broke eye contact with Achim, nor did his smile of welcome waver.

"There were ten, were there not? And all were healed?"

"It seems that you already know, master…."

"Ah, and where are the others? Only you, just one, came back to give thanks?"

"I came alone, master. The others…they are afraid of not following your instructions. But I wondered if you were greater than the priests, and wanted to thank you first."

The man's smile deepened. "You chose well, my son. The others…when they stop being afraid, perhaps they will find me."

"Should I go show myself to the priests, master? Isn't that the Law?"

The man's smile became quizzical. "There is value in following the Law, my son."

"But…the Law did not heal me. You did."

"There is One who is greater than the Law."

Achim stood in the midst of that group, holding onto the hand that was still offered freely to him. He had spent his entire life listening to the stories, and seeking to honor the gods. He still had ended up in the leper's camp. It hadn't banished the lions of disease that had ravaged his body, but with a single word this man returned him to life. This man was greater than the Law, greater than the priests, greater than the idols. Was he perhaps even as great as HaShem, whose temple had caused the lions to flee so many generations ago?

"Who are you? I will follow you…"

The man nodded, tightened his grip, and then released Achim's hand. "Go. Go to the Hebrew temple and show yourself to the priests, so that you may be declared clean in everyone's sight. Give glory to God. Tell the others." He began to move down the road again, and the other men had to pass Achim as they trailed after their leader. The one closest paused before he walked past, and held out his own hand. Achim stared at the man's work-roughened palm for a moment, then at his own newly restored self. He accepted the handclasp with a smile, and the other man smiled back at him.

"I am glad you are well, my brother. God be thanked."

"God be thanked…." repeated Achim, and then realized that was the one thing in his heart, so he shouted. "God be thanked!"

The teacher and healer turned once more, to smile yet again at Achim as the others repeated the simple offering of praise. "God be thanked!....God be thanked!"

No other offering was needed.

ALABASTER

In a small town marketplace, everyone knew nearly everybody else, and Mariam's mother knew more than most. When she walked through the town, men avoided her gaze while women focused fierce eyes on her…so she learned to go to the market during the worst hours. When most people were done with their shopping and socializing, and were back hidden away in shady spaces, Mariam and her mother took care of their own business in the blistering heat. The vegetables may have wilted, the flies may have clustered onto the warm meat, and the bread may have developed the toughness that came with being stale, but it was easier in many other aspects. The men were too tired and hot to harass her or ask for her favors behind their tents in exchange for the goods she sought to buy. The market may have been a sweltering, stink-filled place, but her mother was able to hold her head up and argue prices down like an honest woman.

And this was also how she had bought the jar of pure alabaster. She could have spent night after night turning her head aside while the craftsman had his use of her, and accepted a lesser jar in trade, but something so beautiful and pure deserved to be acquired in a good and honest manner. So she used the only trade she knew to earn each and every one of the dirty coins, smudged with both grime and guilt. She saved them in tiny pouches that she had sewn herself and kept hidden in the thatch of her roof. Once a coin had been lost, and Mariam remembered watching her mother first poke through the thatch, causing bits of straw and chaff to filter down on them, and then sweep the house carefully, bit by bit, until she finally found it lodged in a crack of the dried mud floor. Her eyes shone as she called Mariam over. "Look, daughter--I thought it had been lost, but it has been restored." Her voice was hushed but vibrant. "This is our treasure, my girl, hard earned and carefully kept. Don't tell anyone about it. It's not to be used for the benefit of this life. It has a purpose...and that purpose is greater than anything else we will do while living."

The day when they had gone to the market to purchase the jar was hot and smelled like all the others, but her mother had an unapologetic focus, sharp as a knife edge. She did not meander through the market, but moved directly to the perfumer's stall, dragging Mariam by the hand behind her. The craftsman had several jars on his table, and behind him were larger ones, filled with the most fragrant perfume. He only ever lifted the lid of his large jars for the tiniest crack, letting the merest whiff of scent float out. It had its own holiness, that scent. It was too precious to be used in life, but saved to anoint the dead. Her mother had known for some time which jar she wanted, even though it was not usually set out for view. They had only glimpsed it a few times, and Mariam had noticed the way her mother focused all her attention when it was visible. It truly was a beautiful and delicate thing. Tall and slender like her mother, the jar had graceful lines from its stable base, up around its belly, through the slender neck, and along the wide mouth. The craftsman had made a stopper for it, one that rested neatly on the opening, making it a simple thing to seal with wax. It was already filled with fragrant nard, and even though it was closed, the scent of holiness and beauty hung in a cloud about it. That cloud pushed back the rest of the stench of the market, and in this one corner there was the peace that came with something pure. Mariam was familiar with the scented oils her mother sometimes used, but the nard was the smell of the holy temples and of the attempts to make the dead beautiful.

The craftsman, however, was not part of that purity. He had a knowing sneer on his face as Mariam and her mother approached, an expression that made Mariam hide behind her mother's skirts. "Well….come to make arrangements? I may have something of clay for you, scented oil all the way from olive groves in Jerusalem, but I will want…err…payment as soon as the heat of the day has abated."

"No." Her mother, used to being afforded a measure of dignity this time of day, was angry. She held back from letting it show too much; future business was still important, but neither did she let her lowliness of life deter her. "I know what I want, and I am prepared to pay...as long as you charge a reasonable price." While her words were calm, the sun was not the only thing that threatened to blister the face of the craftsman.

He had no answer to this woman who was suddenly behaving so oddly. His dealings with her had been much more straightforward in the past, and he wasn't quite sure what to do. He tapped a finger on his counter as he waited.

"I wish to look more closely at your alabaster jars. Bring them forward."

Mariam knew that her mother had the one specific jar in mind, but that she needed to go through the proper process. The craftsman, with a bit of a smile, turned around towards some of the wares behind him, out of common reach. That smile was still lingering as he set three small, cream-colored boxes on the cloth in front of this preposterous woman. Her mother made a swift glance over all three, and waved her hand.

"Do you think I have no judgement? Not only are these poorly made, and out of flawed alabaster, but I'm sure that you are thinking of charging me far more than they're worth. And that one is already about to crack. I'm not a fool...find me something that is actually worth purchasing."

The nasty smile was still there, but now the craftsman added an uplifted eyebrow as he turned to replace the boxes, and then reached for some other vessels.

"Those are better. The alabaster is still not your best, but the work is better," said her mother. "Do you have any that are made of a more pure material?"

Now the smile was gone, and the craftsman began to frown. "Be sure you are not wasting my time, mistress….and also be sure that if your brat tries to steal from me, I will bring the fullness of the law upon you."

"Oh, have no fear of either of those, just show me something better." Her mother had a back that was strong and straight, and Mariam smiled out of pride for the dignity that her mother was able to muster.

This time, the craftsman turned about holding four small leather bags in his hands. One by one, he loosened the drawstrings and pulled out the jars. His hands were slow and reverent as he set each lovingly upon the counter, letting their beauty speak for themselves.

"Here they are, mistress, fine alabaster, carved well. Some of the finest in Samaria…but how might you think of paying for these? None of your favors are equal to the price of any."

Her mother, not taking her eyes off of the line on the counter, reached into the folds of her cloak and pulled out a pouch, larger than the ones Mariam had seen before. "I can pay."

The craftsman let out a short bark of a laugh. "You can pay! Mistress, these are the best….you would not find better in Jerusalem, not even in Rome! These each would cost more than a year's wages for an honest man, much less a wh--"

"I can pay. Now tell me your prices."

Mariam usually enjoyed this part, when the seller and her mother entered a complicated game of words, balancing quality and rejection. This time, however, the game never began. The craftsman only showed anger and began to put one jar back into its bag, and not as gently as he had gotten them out, either.

"I will not trade with you. These are too fine for a sinful woman like you. Even if I were to have pity and lower the price to two hundred fifty denarius--an unheard-of price-- you would never be able to buy it."

"Two hundred fifty? For which one? If I had that money, you would sell one?"

The craftsman's hands froze in the process of replacing a jar. Mariam could tell that her mother was trying to not seem too focused, but it was the one jar she had looked for every time they had passed the stall. It was the smallest of them all, but the lines were perfect. The alabaster was so pure that it seemed lit from within, glowing gently even in the harsh mid-day sun. They all gazed at it, appreciating the beauty of something so lovely, as it was cradled in the man's knobby and knuckled hands.

"This one. I would consider selling this one for two hundred fifty denarius. But, woman…"

"I have it. Here. Count carefully." Mariam's mother opened the drawstring of her own pouch, and began to stack her coins in neat piles on the counter next to the other two jars. The craftsman remained immobile, his eyes narrowing as he followed the progress of the coins from pouch to pile, observing the regularity of each. He had the restraint to not begin biting each coin to test it for counterfeit, but let the observation of his eyes be enough of a test. After an eternity filled only by the motion of the woman's hands and the sound of coins being stacked, the piles were completed.

"Do you wish to count them for yourself?"

Her low voice broke the immobility of the craftsman, and he lifted his eyes to look her directly in the face for the first time since she had approached his table. "I can see that the full price is paid, mistress." He slid the jar into its bag, and gently pulled the drawstring shut. "It is already filled with pure nard. I had always thought it would go to the fine villa of a Roman, but--" his mouth barely moved as he muttered the words "--may you have joy of it." The outline of the jar was still seen through the leather of the pouch as it rested in the man's cupped hands. He extended his arms and offered Mariam's mother the beautiful thing, and after she lifted it up, he reached under his counter for his coin box, gently and swiftly sweeping the piles of money into it. Mariam watched as her mother placed the jar in its bag into her own larger pouch, and it no longer looked deflated. It was filled with the hidden riches of that beauty.

"I give you my thanks, craftsman. Remember me to your good wife." The craftsman flinched and looked away in the avoidance that Mariam was used to seeing on the faces of some of the better men. It was the last time that either of them ever saw that craftsman--which was quite the feat in their village. But they never again went to the corner of the market where he kept his stall, and he never again came to their house.

When they arrived back at their tiny hut, they were spent from the heat. They both took a moment to set aside their more commonplace purchases of the day, then her mother moved the short stool far from the lone window, and sat with the new little bag on her lap. The air was thick with heat, and her hands moved slowly through the thickness to loosen the string and draw out the jar. A mere whiff of scent clung to the alabaster, although the wax seal was visible in a complete ring under the stopper. Her mother held it close before her and curled her back around it, shielding it from view of the window. She cupped it in both hands just as the craftsman had done. Once again the lovely thing seemed to give off a gentle light of its own, almost radiant in the dim shadows of the room. Her mother gazed at the treasure in her hands for long minutes before speaking.

"I am a whore, and the daughter of a whore," she murmured to herself, "and I do not have fathers to be gathered to when I die, but may my mothers receive me. May the Father God of all let the scent of this perfume cover the stench of my sins, and let me be gathered in."

She lifted her head and looked at Mariam. "Come here, my girl…" Mariam came closer and reached out a single finger to lightly stroke the smooth, glowing alabaster. Her mother watched without expression as the girl was drawn in to the beauty of the jar and the gentle cloud of scent around them both. "In his wisdom, King Solomon said that a righteous man gathers wealth for his children and his children's children. I am not righteous, but our Lord has seen fit to allow us to have this wealth, and used properly, it will anoint me at the time of my death, it will anoint you, and it will anoint a child of yours as well. No matter what our lives are, at our deaths we will find honor."

She paused to just breathe a moment, and then lifted her head to watch the specks of dust float in the streams of sunlight shining through the shutters. "The priests say that the true God cannot look upon unrighteousness, and for us….such as we are, there is a great deal of that to see. But in Jerusalem, they use incense at the Temple to cover sins so that the priest won't die as he approaches the altar, and perhaps this perfume will cover our sins and let us be accepted past the grave. No matter what our lives are, at our deaths we will find honor. This is our treasure. We will keep it safe, and we will tell no one. When I die, use only a little of the perfume in it. Make sure that you keep the greater portion safe and secure in the jar. Not a drop is to be wasted. This life….there is little justice and little goodness for such as we are, but perhaps in death we might find entry to something better." Mariam looked solemnly at her mother's face, and they understood each other. The jar with its perfume of purity and holiness was their hope.

Through the years they kept it safe, tucked in the rushes of the roof as the coins had been. There were pouches of coins again, but they were not hoarded with such care as before. Every so often, when she thought Mariam was asleep, her mother reached into the rushes to find the little bag, pull out the jar, and breathe the scent of the nard that infused the wax seal as she allowed herself to be drawn in to its beauty. And then, when she became sick and her breath began to rattle in her chest, she made sure that Mariam knew precisely where the alabaster jar was hidden.

"I may not be with you much longer, daughter. And when that time comes, it will be time to use the perfume. This is the one thing I have to help me find a hope past death, and you must bring it when I say it is time." Mariam had looked in her mother's face, scared at the peaks and valleys she noticed for the first time across her cheeks. It didn't bear to be thought about, but she silently nodded, and set her heart to hope that she would not need to pull the pouch down out of the rushes soon.

But it was only days afterward that her mother was unable to get off of her cot. She tried to push herself up, but her arms gave way beneath her and she fell back. Mariam brought her a drink of water. It was the last in the jar from the day before, tepid and stale, and her mother took a small sip before waving it away. She rested back in exhaustion from those simple motions, then used her fading energy to motion at the hiding place of the jar.

Mariam understood, and dragged the stool across the room so she could climb up on it and reach into the rushes. It took her a moment to find the leather pouch and pull it down carefully. She dragged the stool over to her mother's bed, and held the pouch gently on her knees. "I am here, *Imma*. What do you need?"

Her mother worked to pull in enough air. "O….pen."

Mariam's fingers had suddenly lost their skill and gave her trouble in untying the laces. It took some time before she was able to pull out the jar, still glowing with its own purity, and hold it upright so her mother could see it well.

There was another painful inhale, and another word floated out on her failing breath. "Knife…."

Mariam fumbled again as she pulled her small knife out of her own pouch. Her mother waved once more at the jar and used another precious breath to repeat "o….pen."

Mariam hesitated this time. This was their treasure, their hope of being acceptable to the great God in their death. Lifting the wax to break the seal of the jar was an act of finality, and meant things that Mariam didn't want to face. Her mother used even more strength to reach out and tap the top of the jar with some impatience. She pulled more air into her lungs, and repeated "o-pen. I want…to smell."

Mariam held her knife and gently set it along the wax that held the stopper onto the jar. Her hands still had difficulty obeying her and they were clumsy and weak. But her mother watched with burning eyes, and Mariam's knife began to find passage under the wax. She gradually eased the blade in between the wax seal and the polished alabaster. It was slow work, as she pried away the lid, anxious not to damage the precious jar itself. Twice her knife slipped, and the fire in her mother's eyes burned hotter. Each time a bit of wax fell off, Mariam carefully picked it up and set it on the pouch so that she could use it later to re-seal the jar, when her need for the perfume had ended. And with each little sliver of wax, Mariam found herself moving more slowly, reluctant to complete this task. Her hands still seemed as if they had their own life and were also reluctant to face what was happening in this small hut.   She did not want this perfume to be needed, and even more so, did not want the need to be over and past.   But she forced herself to work faithfully and well, and far too soon the last bit of wax lifted and she was able to pull the stopper clear of the narrow neck.

Neither of them were prepared for the glory that poured out and filled the room.   Unhindered, the scent of the nard shimmered in their dusky firelight, causing them both to widen their eyes and look about.   Surely angels attended to a scent like that.   Her mother's breathing became less noisy, and her eyes had an edge of peace to them.

"An-oint me….daught...er."   Mariam silently covered the mouth of the jar with her thumb, and tipped it until she could feel the coolness of the perfume on her skin.   Gently, she reached out to her mother's right earlobe.

"May you hear the welcome of our God."

She leaned towards her mother's right thumb.

"May you have a place in His Kingdom."

She lifted the bed covering and touched her mother's large toe on her right foot.

"May you hasten to glory with peace."

Her mother lay back with her eyes closed, drinking in the beauty in the very air about her.   Her breathing was

even quieter now and more peaceful, and for a moment
Mariam hoped wildly that they had been too soon, that the
breaking of the seal had been a mistake. A glorious
mistake, and not one they would regret, but perhaps a truly
unneeded act. Her mother lifted her hand to her face,
inhaling deeply of the nard on her fingers. She had been
breathing shallowly before, and as she worked hard to pull
the air deeper into her lungs, Mariam could hear the rattle
again. The very sound was painful, and the pain of it killed
the hope that this might be an illness that would pass with
anything short of death. Mariam sat and waited, watching
the spots of sunlight pass along the floor through the day.
Eventually the light faded and shadows filled the room.
The darkness became as thick as the smell of the nard, and
normally would have filled Mariam with fear. However,
tonight even the air was anointed, and the thickness of it
became a support for her mother's soul. Mariam was aware
of the moment when that soul stepped away from its sad
body, became enfolded by the fragrant dark, and was lifted
away. And then the scented darkness wrapped itself around
her, shielding her and comforting her in her solitude.

As the fatherless daughter of a whore, Mariam had no
clout in the community to be able to bury her mother
properly. After doing her best to wrap her mother's body,
she handed over some of her few precious coins to a
neighbor for the use of his cart to transport her. He had
the kindness to merely mutter "may she find rest," and

neither comment on what her place in society had been, nor proposition her daughter. Not yet.

But when the time of mourning was ending, and Mariam had undergone the cleansing to the best of her ability, she found that her coin supply was dwindling. She began to reckon with the fact that she had needs that were likely to continue her whole life. What was the option for the daughter and granddaughter of whores? There was only one way she knew to live and provide for herself. Without thought, and with as little emotion as possible, she began to take up her mother's mantle, and with it the veil of a prostitute. And while she was now the object of fierce glares from women, and no man would meet her eye in the market, she knew that she still had a treasure of purity. Her life may be one thing, but at the end of it, she had hope of being accepted into the Kingdom of God. As it had for her mother, the glory of the scent of nard would be sure to overwhelm the stench of her sins. And through the years, those sins accumulated. The perfume in that bottle of alabaster would need to be holy indeed.

The years carried on and the market never changed; the heat and the smells were Mariam's only experience of it. She learned to barter with the best of them, and keep as many of her precious coins as possible by exclaiming loudly and truthfully about the overpowering stench of the fish. She was in the middle of one such negotiation when there was a ruckus behind her. "I tell you, he knew everything," a female voice was shouting. "Even about you, Tyrek, and yes, you also Yonas! He told me of my whole life as if he knew it better than I did...and he spoke of our God and not of worshipping at the Temple in Jerusalem or worshipping here, but...oh, you need to come see him..."

Mariam recognized Anat, since she was a woman like herself. They had never spoken to each other, but Anat was known as one who tried to leave her position in the village and become an honest wife. But no man would officially marry her, and she had passed from one to the other, always in hope that she would be protected as a wife, always discarded when a proper wife was brought into the home. She was also one who never met the eyes of honest men in the market, and who avoided the public places during the cool mornings. But now, instead of shrinking from notice, Anat was demanding it. Her voice became louder, more sure, and more commanding as she directed the townspeople toward the common well. Mariam found herself swept up in the motion, curious about this man that brought Anat out of her reticence and gave her such open-faced courage. Mariam tugged her own veil firmly in place, shrinking deeper into it and letting herself be just a form, a voiceless member of the crowd.

Anat led them to a man sitting on the edge of the well, who was calmly sipping water and watching the group of villagers approach. He had a few friends approaching from another direction, and one of them handed him a piece of bread as he looked at the crowd curiously. Mariam couldn't hear what the friend asked this man who sat with such stillness, but she saw the shake of the head in reply, the gentle smile, and the movement of the hand as he waved the crowd closer. Mariam stayed in her position along the outer edge of the crowd, but she could still hear as the man greeted the villagers.

One of the elders of the synagogue spoke to him first, and Mariam could tell he had already decided this visitor was unwelcome; his voice was harsh and overly assured. "This woman tells us that you have opinions about how we worship."

The visitor looked at him calmly for a moment, holding his eyes and allowing his stillness to flow over the crowd. "Well, I will tell you something. I was in the Temple in Jerusalem, and saw a good Pharisee come in. He knew his prayers, and he was careful to observe all the law. He stood before the temple and began to pray before giving his offering. 'Blessed are you, Lord God, King of the Universe, who did not make me a sinner,' he said."

The men who were elders, some Pharisees themselves, nodded. They knew that prayer.

The visitor continued. "Then, he lifted his arms higher, and said 'Blessed are you, Lord God, King of the Universe, who did not make me a slave,'"

The leaders of the village eyeballed each other now. It was a common prayer, why was this man focusing on it?

"And of course, after that, he lifted his arms even higher and said, 'Blessed are you, Lord God, King of the Universe, who did not make me a woman.' He then drew several pouches out and carefully and slowly emptied each one for an offering. And far behind him, in the women's court, a widow crept forward and set two tiny *asses* in the bowl for offerings. She offered no great prayer, but gave what she had and whispered "Blessed are you," No one saw her but myself."

The elders and Pharisees were bored now. No one cared about this inconsequential woman.

"She was a true worshipper, while the Pharisee was not."

The entire crowd snapped to attention, and more than one indignantly sucked in air. The shift in attitudes allowed a space to open up in front of Mariam. She drew herself forward to get a better look at this quiet man who was creating such consternation.

He continued. "As I told Anat, the time is coming, and is here even now, when true worshippers are not those who are at the correct temple, reciting the correct prayers, but are worshipping in spirit and in truth."

His head turned, and he looked at Mariam. No man had looked her in the face for as long as she could remember, but he saw past her veil and her obvious standing in the community, and managed to look gently and directly into her eyes. "Are you a true worshipper?" he asked softly, and she knew this question was personal and not meant for the entire crowd.

"Rabbi...I...I am a sinner. I am not fit…."

"God sees the heart, daughter, not the outside. Do you desire to be clean and truly worship?"

"Rabbi...my only hope is to be accepted by God at the end of my life. I….I do wish to be clean.."

"Do you have a cloak...shoes for walking?"

"At my house, Rabbi."

"Go, get them, and then follow me."

Mariam held his eyes for just a moment more. It was so strange to simply be seen with such gentleness. Then, with her head held higher than she had thought possible, she turned and walked back to her hut. Calmly, she found a large sack, and began to bundle things for a journey. She added the bread that she had recently purchased, as well as the dried figs that she'd been saving. She reached into the rushes of the ceiling, pulling down several pouches of coin, and finally the larger pouch with her treasure. She could just catch the hint of scent from the jar, permeating through the leather that enclosed it. This she set in the middle of a blanket and rolled it carefully. It had to be protected above all else. This Rabbi seemed different from any other

Pharisee who taught about how to please God, but she still wanted her assurance that she would be acceptable in God's kingdom when her life ended. But who would be there to anoint her?

Traveling with this new Rabbi was a strange experience. His kindness flowed out like a perfume of his own around those who followed him and became the fragrance of how they each related to one another. Mariam walked alongside other women for the first time since her mother died. And while these women came from such different stations--one even dealt in purple linen and wore her own gold ornaments openly--they worked together without anger or envy. When they found that Mariam had a voice that was true to singing, they often asked her to lead the blessings before meals. Slowly Mariam lost the desire to tuck her chin deeply onto her chest and move about with her eyes fixed firmly on the ground. She held her head up as high as on that day that the teacher invited her to follow him, and she saw the stars emerge while she sat next to the other women. And she got to listen to the Rabbi.

He talked of the Law and the Prophets, mostly, and then talked of what they had meant all along. As he journeyed across the countryside, he used everything--the grass, the birds--to tell his followers of God's love and care for them. He told stories of sinners who were found acceptable in God's eyes, and Mariam wept through those. If a beggar could end up in Abraham's bosom, could the daughter and grand-daughter of whores find her way also? If those who were too poor to make any kind of offering in the temple could still gain entrance to the kingdom of God, perhaps she, with her few bits of coin and her one treasure, would be able to cover the sins of her life. She loved following this man, and the more he taught, the more she loved both him and God together.

As they continued south, steadily moving towards Jerusalem, his teaching started to change. Instead of comfort and love and healing for her heart, the Rabbi began to talk about strange things in the future. He said that he wanted to prepare them for the time when he would not be with them, and some of his closer disciples showed their confusion. "Are you going on a journey without us, Rabbi?" they asked. "We will follow you wherever you lead us...we will not abandon you, Rabbi."

The teacher's eyes grew sad at these assertions, and as he seemed to try to explain what he meant, his followers only got more confused. But Mariam started to wonder. When he spoke of a "time when I will no longer be with you," Mariam heard echoes of her mother's voice. She had known when her death was close before Mariam had understood, and had tried to warn her daughter that that illness would defeat her. Then Mariam had preferred to hope for life, but her hopes were disappointed. Now, her hope was more and more in this Rabbi...and he was using the same words. She even caught him looking directly at her with his gentle gaze while he did so, as if he knew her memories and was trying to give a message just to her.

One evening as the edge of the world still glowed gold and orange, and stars shone in the deep blue directly over her head, he said again, "A little longer, and you will look for me but you will not find me. I will no longer be with you, but take heart, for I have overcome sin and my victory over death will follow." He was turned towards Mariam as he said this, and she pushed past her usual desire to stay quiet to ask softly, "Rabbi, do you mean your own death? My mother spoke that way…."

He held her gaze for a long time as the sky deepened above them. "Have comfort, daughter, I have overcome death and the grave." The gold at the rim of the world faded in the silence after his words, and Mariam watched the rocks and grass at her feet fade with it. When she looked up, she could still see his face turned towards her, and the glimmer of his eyes in the firelight.

"It would take great holiness to completely overcome death, Rabbi," she whispered.

"I have done so, daughter. Do not fear, whatever the future holds. I have already overcome, and you are mine."

"Have you overcome my death, as well?"

She hadn't gotten used to his quietness and stillness yet. It continued to wash over her as if it were new. His way of looking at her was continually surprising--as though he didn't see what she was, but only saw her as a simple woman. As more stars appeared overhead, his voice was quieter than the firelight.

"I have. And where I am, I will make sure to bring you. Only believe, my daughter, and follow me."

"Only?"

"Only believe, and follow me. You need nothing else; no sacrifice, no offering, no covering or perfume, nothing except love. I will carry you with me."

At that, he slowly stood up and moved away, pausing to rest a hand on a child's head as he spoke with the little one's father. His voice was still low, and too quiet for anyone beyond the father and child to hear his words. But Mariam followed him with her eyes as far as she could in the dark, listening to his sandals stepping surely away from her, until he was hidden away in the gloom. Her hand was resting on her bag of belongings, and to her knowing touch, she was able to feel the roll of cloth that sheltered her treasure and what had been her hope of heaven. She believed the words of this quiet man with the core of her heart, and if he, in his holiness, had overcome the grave, what need did she have of her perfume to try to make herself acceptable to the Father? The protection of her alabaster jar had long been the focus of her life, but now she was unsure of its place. She would continue to carry it, but for what end? Thanks be to God, she had no child of her own to curse with her mother's veil, but there was then no one to anoint her at her own death, and perhaps even the need for that anointing was lessened. Her beautiful white jar with its shimmering contents rested under the layers under her hand, waiting for its rightful purpose.

As he stayed a few days by Bethany, things began to change for the group that followed this teacher. More and more crowds appeared, and the Rabbi was invited to dine with all sorts of people.

Sometimes he was invited to a humble home where he was known, and he responded to exuberant greetings with great smiles and embraces of his own. Some of his hosts lived in homes that had housed generations of well respected men, where the law was observed carefully in full view of all, so that there could be no criticism. The Rabbi became somber at these meetings, allowing his host to perform the correct washings and blessings, but there were stories told afterwards about how he caused some significant consternation with a few rather pointed questions. And some were homes of people who were descended from the children of Israel, but who had never worshiped at the Temple, and held the customs of the Law in light regard. They were curious about this gentle teacher who created such a stir, and brought him into their homes as a showpiece. The Rabbi then had quite a few pointed questions aimed towards him, both during those dinners and after, and some were from his own followers. Why would he waste his time and tarnish his reputation by associating with unclean men?

The Rabbi was always quiet for several moments after those questions, allowing the words to reverberate into his stillness. Usually, the one asking would start to turn his head away, frowning as he was bothered by whatever thoughts came to the surface. Nearly every time, they would look back up at the teacher with a question in their eyes, and the Rabbi would smile and nod gently. After a responding nod and a whispered "thank you," the man who had been rough in his righteous indignation would walk away calmly. Mariam, though, never felt a need to lower her head before the Rabbi. Instead, she continued to learn to hold her head up as she walked in this community.

One evening, the Rabbi was invited to the home of a true Pharisee. This man had sent a servant to do the inviting, and he stood before the Rabbi as the sun set and the clouds caught the gold of the horizon. He may have been just a servant, but he was dressed in more wealth than Mariam had ever owned altogether. Mariam was glad of the shadows to hide in, able to observe this man without drawing any attention to herself. He approached the Rabbi with confidence, and was obviously used to keeping his back straight and his own head high. He was not there to beseech, but to extend the invitation of his master with an air of a summons. The teacher's mouth quirked upwards more than once as the servant delivered his carefully prepared words, and then he asked gently "Shall I follow you to the home of your master now?"

The servant stepped back slightly, a bit nonplussed by the gentle acquiescence. He had obviously expected a bit more ceremony on accepting such an honorable invitation. But he was well versed in his own manners, and simply said "whenever you are ready, *Mar,* I will lead you to my master's house."

"Oh, I am ready. I have been awaiting your master's message, and I have no preparations to make."

The servant looked at the humble tunic and well-worn sandals. Neither were necessarily rags, but for such an important house, surely there were better robes somewhere….While he said nothing, his consternation was clear on his face. The teacher's mouth quirked upwards again.

"I am as I am, my son. And I am prepared to dine with your master...as I am."

Mariam had enjoyed watching this entire exchange immensely. The servant had nothing left to do except pivot and begin to walk back to his master's house. He did turn back once, in the hopes of a bit more ceremony--and therefore honor for both him and his position in a great man's home. The Rabbi was close on his heels, though, and obviously planning to continue walking, so the only option was to turn his face again and continue back. Mariam could see just that twitch of a smile once more on her Rabbi's face as he began to walk past her. She couldn't help but smile a bit on her own, and the teacher met her eyes, letting himself enjoy the shared humor. Then, the fun in his own eyes faded away, and he became very grave and still.

"It will be soon, daughter. Be prepared, and remember that I have overcome death, and where I go, I will make sure you come."

Mariams's bag suddenly became too heavy for her to carry, and she lowered it into the dust at her feet as she watched the back of her Rabbi walk away from her. She didn't want the kindness and gentleness of this man to go out of her life, not this evening, not ever. She had packed a few belongings and left her home so that she could follow his footsteps, and now this heavy bag was all that she had left to abandon. He said he would be sure to bring her wherever he went. Did that mean this night, as well? She glanced down at her bag again, and at her surroundings, and decided that nothing was as important as following her teacher for as long as she was able. And yet...he had made it clear that he would be leaving soon, and that the task in front of him was overcoming death. If he were going to battle death itself, he needed to have all the preparation and readiness he could; he needed to be anointed before that battle. He was already a good man, but death was the one enemy that had always been invincible. She had no holiness of her own to offer, and no wealth to make offerings on his behalf, but she had her one treasure, the one thing that she had pinned her own hopes of heaven upon, and she could use that to anoint him...

After these moments of standing frozen and worried, she was suddenly panic-stricken at the thought of being separated from her teacher at all, even if just for an evening. Her lovely alabaster jar and its exquisite contents became nothing but a burden when she thought of the love she had seen in that one man's eyes. She knelt down in the dust and fumbled at the drawstring of her bag, reaching deep into it and pulling the roll of cloth out, scattering her other belongings in her haste. She used a bit more care as she quickly unrolled the cloth to get to the little pouch in the middle. As soon as she could feel the smooth lines of her jar through the soft leather, she pushed away everything else, leaving her nearly empty bag and its scattered contents in the dust where they had dropped. She almost tripped on the hem of her own robe as she stood up and began to follow that pompous servant and the calm man behind him. He was now her hope of heaven, and if he was going to battle death, out of her love she wanted to give him her only weapon against that struggle.

No one noticed her as she followed; there was such focus on her teacher that she was able to stay at the back of the group of invited guests as they entered the house of the Pharisee. One servant began to approach her with a tray of bread, assuming she was there to help with the feast, but Mariam simply shook her head and waved in a general manner at the men washing their hands. The other servant seemed to accept that as a sign that she was attached to one of the guests for some reason, and left her alone.

Mariam didn't dare draw her jar out of the pouch with so many people about, for she was sure that there would quickly be questions for how a humble woman had such a treasure in her possession. But perhaps she could find a way to give it to him once the diners had finished their washing and began to move through the house. She quietly opened the pouch but kept the jar within, held close to her side. This was her chance to be the least obtrusive and disruptive--if she were to make an offering of her one treasure, she could do so without fuss before everyone moved into the main room and sat down. They were distracted now, and she might be able to move through the group to her Rabbi and give him her gift in a way that would not seem remarkable. There was a chance, if she was quick, that they would also mistake her for a servant and not pay any attention to her presence at all.

She slid her hand into the pouch, now pulling the jar out but trying to keep it covered by her sleeve, and glanced down quickly to make sure it wasn't too noticeable. It had been some time since she had unwrapped the jar and looked at it. The round base and graceful, long neck were as they had always been, but the beauty of it struck her anew. Through her years of dishonor, nothing had touched the purity of the alabaster. It still caught the light in a way that made it seem to glow, and the merest hint of the scent of the nard held within still floated about it. She let herself forget to be cautious for just a moment and cupped it with both hands once more to get a final look at it. While she paused in the midst of all the movement and breathed deeply, she then realized that when she had left everything else behind her in the dust, she had also left her knife. She had no tool to pry the wax seal open, and now every moment was precious.

One by one, the men were finishing their washings and moving on, her dear teacher in the midst of them all. She looked about, searching for anything that was thin and strong enough to lift up the wax, but could see nothing useful in that fine hall. She scraped at the wax with her fingernails, watching one more man and then another move through the doorway. In her haste, the scrapings fell on the mosaic floor, flecks of tawny beeswax dotting the tiles. After working her way around the neck of the jar, she pulled on the top in hope that it would perhaps move at least a little. But the stopper was on tight and she could not get to enough of the wax to allow it to move.

She tried warming the neck of the bottle in her hands-- beeswax was malleable enough when it was warm--and once again pulled on the top, twisting it a little to get it to move. In a moment of joy, the top of the lid finally came away in her hand. But that joy was brief--she was suddenly horrified as she realized that it was the knob only, and that the rest of the stopper was still in the neck of the jar, sealed tight with beeswax all around it. In her haste, she had used too much strength for the stopper and broken it. And in her childhood grief at her mother's deathbed, she had sloppily used too much wax to seal her jar. There was no way now to lift up a simple rim of wax and release the stopper. It was fused together with the neck into one impervious length, blocking the precious nard from flowing out.

As Mariam froze with her sealed alabaster jar in one hand, and the broken knob in the other, the last of the men moved into the dining room and she could hear the house settling into quiet expectation. One man's voice, surely the host, rose into well-measured tones. He gave a greeting to his guests and welcomed this Rabbi, but he used words and tone to indicate that he was skeptical about any good coming from the humble man seated at his table. Meanwhile Mariam still stood in the entryway, wondering if she should just go back to the hill where the rest of the followers were resting for the evening. She shouldn't have left her bag on the ground like that--hopefully it was still there and she could pack everything back away. If she spent some time on it, she may be able to chisel the wax out from around the stopper and find a way to release it without losing much of the perfume inside. A new stopper could be made….while she deliberated, the host's words filtered through the doorway to her.

"...one who has spoken much about the kingdom of God, and that is surely something we all wish to see. However, if I may, sir, you don't seem to be very active in preparing to finally bring that kingdom to fruition. For certain, we are all tired of being ruled and occupied by gentiles. The Romans may not be quite as bad as the Hasmoneans, but still, the people of God ought to have their own land and be ruled by actual and direct descendants of David. And you say you are such, are you not? I am sure all gathered here would appreciate hearing your lineage, and what your plans are...."

There was silence throughout the house, filtering out to Mariam as guests and servants alike waited to hear how they would be liberated from Roman rule and their nation re-created as free people. In the quiet, a few shifted their position, and Mariam could hear a glass lifted, drunk from, and set down. And then her Rabbi's voice flowed out into the air.

"My kingdom," he said, "is not of this world, but in the hearts of those who follow me."

The consternation he caused with these words also flowed into the air. There was an increase in the sound of shuffling, a few sounds of "hem" as men cleared their throats, the sound of several more cups being lifted and drunk from. This wasn't the clear answer they had looked for. Mariam lifted her head and stared at the doorway, as if she could look past the wall and to the place where the teacher sat. He had told her that he had overcome death...his kingdom was surely beyond anything those men were thinking, and if the time was near for him to move into that victory, she just didn't want to wait to offer him her treasure. Going back to the camp wasn't the right choice. She didn't think that he needed the assistance of the perfume to make him appear holy to the Father, but his own holiness made the beauty of the nard right and fitting...like being drawn to like. And his time was close. She couldn't go back to her bag just yet.

In an instinctual movement, she adjusted her veil to hide her face, not wanting to be seen by the men around that table. She had worn her veil that way for so long as she moved through the village seeking to support herself that it was almost a comfort to hide within it. As she moved into the dining room, she could hear an increase in the shuffling of the guests, a few gasps as her clothes made her former livelihood apparent. Someone who had already enjoyed the wine deeply called to the host "Entertainment? I didn't think you were the type!" and grew silent with a grunt as he was glared at. But through all of the other men's reactions, her teacher looked at *her*. He saw her and she knew that in his eyes she was whole and precious and worthy of respect. She held her jar in both hands before her, and she looked at it once more with its complete grace, the lines curving perfectly... a thing that was beautiful in itself. She glanced at her teacher again, and he nodded with a slight smile. He understood.

She had to disregard all the customs that were typical for such gatherings. She did not even acknowledge the host, and she ignored the pompous servant who was hovering off to the side. She kept her eyes on her Rabbi as she approached the table, and his quiet smile gave her courage. She set the neck of her bottle against the edge of the table, and reached for the first solid, heavy thing that she could find. There was a hefty pottery cup close by, and her fingers held it tight. She struck the cup against the uplifted neck of the alabaster jar, and it snapped completely off. The solid mass of jar, wax, and stopper clattered to the ground as the perfume inside began to dribble out. She had been so cautious when she used it for her mother that the jar was still nearly full, and she moved quickly to where the Rabbi's feet rested.

As she poured the nard out onto his feet, the smell of the perfume filled the room. Before, the smells had been a mix of wine and meat and spices, but now the beauty of the fragrance overcame it all. It moved through the air like a living thing, and the shuffling and grunting of offended men was stilled. All of her world became condensed in her master's feet. He loved her without care for what she had been, and without making use of her. He alone was holy enough to overcome her greatest enemy, and he promised that he would be her means of entering a kingdom beyond the sinfulness of this one. She had no more hope in the perfume making her acceptable, but it was right that he should be anointed with it. So she poured it all out on his feet, and when she realized that she had nothing with which to wipe up the excess, she pulled her scarf off of her head-- causing the flummoxed men to come out of their silence and once again begin a concert of disapproving noises--and used her own hair to wipe his feet. With ridiculous boldness, she then reached up and poured the last of the perfume on his very head. As it ran down into his beard, he turned his face towards her. Some remarks of protest were being made around the table--a woman! A sinful woman! And that expensive jar destroyed! The money that could have been used!--but her Rabbi held her eyes with his own acceptance and love.

Her heart was filled to overflowing, and as she stood there, his love became an assurance and hope that was greater than the judgement of her mother's veil, and swept away the disapproval of men better than her. She had complete security in this love, and the release she felt overwhelmed her. She hid her face with her hands as she cried for joy, but when the Rabbi spoke, she lowered them to be able to see him better. After what she had just done, what did it matter if the other men saw her weeping?

"Be at peace, my daughter," he told her. "You have done a good and beautiful thing. From this love, your sins are forgiven and you are clean. No alabaster will match your purity in the kingdom of God."

She knelt at his feet again, the scent of the nard lifting from his whole self and her own hair. She had meant to give all of the perfume to him, but through her service that perfume had become a part of her, as well. "Holiness to the Lord," she breathed into the scented air, "I am the maidservant of the Lord." He rested his hand on her bare head, and she rested in both the hope and the acceptance that he gave.

SERVE

"Yosef was brought down to Mitzrayim. Potifar, an officer of Pharaoh, the captain of the guard, a Mitzrian, bought him from the hand of the Yishme`elim that had brought him down there.…Yosef found favor in his sight. He ministered to him, and he made him overseer over his house, and all that he had he put into his hand."

Pallu stood in the doorway, watching the road, as he recited his favorite verses. Yosef, all those many and many years ago, had been unjustly sold into slavery just as Pallu himself. But Yosef found favor with the Lord God, and in so doing, found favor with his master, and rose to a high position. Pallu could see him, standing in outlandish Egyptian garb, essentially as much a master of the house as the actual master. Pallu typically dismissed the ease with which Yosef had been tossed into jail on the claims of just one woman. The ways of Israel, being God's own people, were obviously far superior to the godless Egyptians, and it would take the testimony of *two* women to let any accusation stand against him. It wasn't the fault of either Yosef or a sign of disfavor from the Almighty that he had been jailed so easily…it was simply the fault of ignorant Egyptian law. And even that couldn't keep Yosef down; as soon as he was released, was he not elevated to an even higher position? God's favor was obvious, and instead of having to do menial work, Yosef moved about freely, collecting wealth and living in his own house. Truly, God approved of Yosef, and he approved of Pallu, as well. Although Pallu had lost his freedom, God had shown his favor in the way he had placed Pallu in authority over the other servants of the house. God was with him. God would be with him. He would rise like Yosef.

"Two days until the feast…" he murmured, and as he mused over the work still to be done, he caught sight of one of the servants, a new boy whose name he just hadn't cared to learn yet. The boy was passing by the corner of the house, and Pallu snapped to sharp focus. "Have you completed your tasks for the preparations for the feast?"

The boy had a bundle of firewood on his back, and he was leaning far forward to be able to balance the large load. He turned his head sideways, and for a moment looked like the hunchback who begged down by the pool. "I've not been able to do much else beyond the firewood, *Mar*. It takes so much to keep the fires going through the Feast so that they don't have to be rekindled…."

Pallu, still seeing Yosef ruling with magnificence in Egypt, crossed his arms and tapped his foot much as the son of Ya'akov would have. "But there is more that must be done! Do not make excuses as to why you are not completed yet. Instead, work harder."

The boy turned his face back down towards his own feet, and Pallu was not able to see his expression. There was a tenseness about his jaw, however, that hinted at an undesirable attitude. Pallu, his arms still folded tightly, set his shoulders firmly down and lifted both his chest and his chin. He must be like Yosef, or he would be nothing. "This must be done by mid-day, do you understand? No more delay."

The boy did not lift his face at all. "Yes, *Mar.*" Without waiting for official dismissal, he moved away beneath his load of wood, and Pallu saw again the form of that despicable hunchback. He sniffed at the association and straightened his own back once more. As the burdened boy continued to move off, Pallu suddenly called after him: "What of the lamb?"

The boy paused, but he was barely able to get the breath to call back. "It is well--I'll make sure the master will be pleased with the lamb's care after I do the firewood!" Pallu thought of how slowly the boy moved under his load. If the master came to check on the lamb and perform his daily inspection, and there was any lack of food or water, he would not think to blame the boy. No, he would turn to his most trusted servant and ask why his trust in this most important task was not fulfilled. He would notice any imperfection in the care of the lamb more than he would notice problems in the rest of the preparations--wine could always be slightly watered, after all--so the lamb's welfare had to be attended to. Pallu grunted and stared at the bottom of the door frame for a moment before heading off to the corner of the house where the lamb was penned in.

It was always a bit of a trial, following the part of the Law's instructions to keep the lamb in the house for four days to be observed. Besides the fact that having an animal in the house also brought in the stench of the stable, there was always tension knowing that the carefully chosen lamb might be found insufficient during that length of time. Once half of the four days had passed, it would be so difficult to either find another suitable animal or make preparations to join extended family for the Feast. Pallu remembered the lamb he'd had once, long ago before injustice had stricken him, which had fallen over in a faint on day four. He had only just gotten that lamb at great expense to himself, and had been sure it was unblemished. However, when it fainted...he'd had to look away and say that, certainly, the fire was too hot and who wouldn't faint in such heat? Certainly, the lamb was still healthy and in its wits, and wasn't the wool pure and white? Certainly it was still acceptable as an offering. And he'd offered it, and injustice was brought against him, and now he served in this house instead of mastering his own. But he would follow all the law and the master's instructions perfectly, and God would again look upon him in favor, and he would continue to rise in importance and control.

And so this lamb must be perfect. Pallu must ensure that the care of the lamb was without fault. He must have God's favor, so he could be like Yosef.

As Pallu got to the corner where the lamb was tethered, he fought against turning his face away from the smell. No, it certainly wasn't pleasant having an animal live right in the house. The straw would need to be changed quickly, but at least the Feast was just a day away, and this would be over for another year. He felt the side of the lamb's dish of water, and was pleased that it felt clean. The lamb had been nibbling at the hay in the manger they'd brought in for him, but paused at Pallu's entrance. It had a single stalk hanging out of its mouth, and it didn't seem bothered by it at all as it gazed placidly at Pallu. Pallu was always so careful that crumbs did not fall into his beard, but this lamb was too foolish to even notice a straw sticking out from under its top lip. Well, he thought, it doesn't have to be intelligent, just unblemished. The Lord has his own purposes.

As he watched the lamb continue to chew, wobbling that lone straw up and down, he heard footsteps and the setting down of a burden behind him. He took a moment to check that he was in order himself, so that his dignity was still secure. Ruth was at the back of the room adjusting a jar of oil. Surely she also was ensuring that preparations for the feast were well in order for her brother's household.

After lifting the lid on another jar and looking at the contents, she straightened and met his gaze.

"Ah, old idler...overseeing things well? Can you oversee the care of that lamb and change the straw so the stink does not stain our stew?"

Pallu tried to find another fingerbreadth or two of height, and frowned at this woman. Would she never learn to treat him with the respect he was owed?

"I have instructed the boy to do so."

"Mm. Yes, I'm sure he'll be able to get right to it after he delivers all the wood. Meanwhile, be sure to check your portion of stew before eating so that it does not contain any of the lamb's own offerings."

Pallu frowned at her more fiercely. He knew from long experience that it was generally worthwhile to appease whatever woman was in charge of the kitchen, but this particular woman...she was not mistress of the house, and therefore her position was less than his. Everything in him choked over the words that he growled out. "Perhaps I will do the boy a favor and change the straw for the lamb."

Ruth kept her face still, but her eyes glimmered unpleasantly. "That would show great wisdom, I believe. I know that the care of the lamb is my brother's highest concern these days."

"As it is mine." Pallu kept his chin up as he passed by Ruth and went to the stable to collect a shovel and bucket, and do the work that was not even his to do. The donkey heard him coming, and brayed out a greeting as he entered the stable. Pallu liked this donkey. His rich brown coat reminded Pallu of freshly turned earth, and his muzzle was as white as creamy goat milk. Pallu paused briefly, grateful for something to keep him from the ridiculous work of shoveling the lamb's dirty straw, and scratched behind the donkey's ears. The young animal snorted and closed his eyes, leaning his head into the friendly hand. After a moment of enjoyment, he stomped a hoof and nudged the gate of his pen.

"I know, I know….you want to go on a journey today, don't you, my friend? Well, we've not got the time for the market, but perhaps I can find you a bit of grass and a carrot." He reached for the head rope and slipped it over the donkey's muzzle and ears before lifting the pin for the gate. Pallu had been training the donkey carefully, making sure that each excursion had been a pleasant one for him. He knew well the stubborn nature shared by all such animals, so every time he led the donkey out or put a small burden on his back, he had been careful to give a reward as well. He'd worked their way up to strapping small baskets with light loads over the donkey's back, and while the donkey had side-eyed that with suspicion, the handful of carrots and grain distracted him from balking. And at the market, since the donkey was of a social turn, Pallu made sure the children were allowed to pet him, and that small treats from various stalls frequently made their way to the soft muzzle.

And so now, the donkey was always happy to oblige when he thought he was going for a nice walk. First he bent his head for the rope, then waited politely for the gate to be fully opened. He walked next to Pallu with a bit of a bounce in his step as they exited the stable, then paused outside the door, ready for the blanket, baskets, and handful of treats. Pallu tugged at the rope, trying to get the donkey to keep moving. But now the donkey chose to show his stubborn nature. He intended to go on a walk and see other people, and he knew that he must carry things in order to get to do so. He snorted and stamped and half-lidded his eyes at Pallu in his impatience to get everything settled.

"Well, friend, today it's either back in or under the tree. Which would you have?" Pallu made a movement as if to lead the donkey back into the dim stable, and the animal set his hooves more firmly into the baked earth beneath him. When Pallu changed directions and moved towards the tree at the corner of the house, the donkey huffed in resignation and chose to follow--but only after one more tug on the rope. Pallu was fully aware that this was the donkey's second choice, but the animal was intelligent enough to know that grazing under a tree was much nicer than being locked in a small pen in the stable. Besides, if it all worked out well, Pallu could get the boy to change the straw in the donkey's pen, and he would go back to a clean and sweet space. Cleaning the donkey's pen was much worse than cleaning the lamb's corner, and Pallu smiled at the thought. If he had to do work that was beneath him, at least there was worse work still to be done by a servant in an even lower station.

Pallu watched the donkey begin to contentedly graze in the pleasant shade under the trees, and wished he could settle there himself for a companionable hour. But he needed to make sure that the boy was still working, and there was still the lamb...after so many days of careful care, he couldn't let that slip on this last day. With a sigh so deep it turned into a grunt, he headed back into the stable to get what he needed to clean out the lamb's corner.

Ruth had made herself conveniently absent while he started this menial work. By the time he had hitched up his robe and broken a sweat, though, she came in with yet another jar, but picked up an empty one and exited quickly before he could pass any of the tasks on to her. He knew she was likely smirking at the sight of him scraping up sodden straw as she left. It did not make either the task or his temper any more pleasant.

He had just set the basket of old straw outside the door, and had refilled the lamb's food when a firmer step announced Meshullam's entrance. As master of the house, he walked freely and with confidence. Pallu winced at the memory of entering his own house with such a step, before he lost the favor of God. He stood, waiting to see what would be said, trying to look worthy of respect. He was so relieved that Meshullam had not entered while he had been actually doing the work of cleaning up after the lamb; perhaps he could avoid admitting that he'd had to stoop to that task himself.

Meshullam smiled through his expansive beard. "Well, Pallu, it seems we are almost ready. I saw the boy readying firewood, Ruth tells me that the stores are in place for the kitchen, and the lamb? You have cared well for him, have you not?"

Pallu grunted as he searched for the right words. "I have ensured that he has had proper care. His food has been well provided, he has been kept clean and comfortable."

Meshullam crouched down in front of the lamb, who was again chewing on his hay. The golden eyes with their wide rectangular pupils turned briefly at Meshullam, and then looked back at the small trough they had brought in for it. Meshullam rested his large hand on the lamb's head. "Well, small friend, for one more year you will be the reminder to Ha Shem that we remember him and ask his forbearance over our sins. It is hard for you, is it not, that it is your blood which is to do so? Yet better your blood than the blood of my brothers or my sons….and may your blood also remind the Lord that his people are oppressed, may he choose to deliver us as he has done before." The lamb continued to focus on the food in front of it, but after another moment it lifted its tail and deposited fresh piles on the floor. Meshullam wrinkled his nose at the smell, then turned to Pallu with half of a smile.

"It is good that you are here and ready, Pallu. It wouldn't do to let the lamb step in that. I'll let you get back to your work as you clean that up." Meshullam exited quickly, and Pallu was left with a burning face. It was still so accepted that he would be the one to do such a task! "I have not earned your complete favor yet, have I, Lord God? Well, if there is even a little of your favor upon me, at least let me finish this in privacy, and don't let anyone see." In spite of his haste, however, Ruth walked back in with yet another jar just as he was carrying the newly soiled straw out. Her smile was not one of friendliness.

"Well done, Pallu. It is good that you are caring so well for the lamb. Try not to let it get as messy as it was this morning, though, eh?"

This was insufferable. "Look, woman! I will ensure that things are done well, it is not my place to do this myself, but if you or the boy are inept, those who are above you must do your work for you!"

Ruth smiled more greatly now. Her voice had hard edges to it. "Of course….*Mar.* How grateful we are that you are assisting us so well."

There was no response to be made. Both Pallu and Ruth knew the intent behind the words, but to argue with the words themselves was impossible. Pallu worked to control a long exhale through his nose, attempting to hide his frustration. After a long moment regarding the floor, he straightened his shoulders again and looked up.

"I am going to the upper room to ensure all is ready for the Feast. I will be back for my mid-day meal afterwards. Do not water the wine overmuch." He did not give her a chance to reply in either refusal or agreement, but turned and went out the door.

The stairs to the upper portion of the house were along the outer wall, and Pallu was careful to stop at a water jar first. So much work had already gone towards the care and cleaning of the room, and he did not want to sully it. Although it was not time for a meal, he still performed the full seven handwashings, and after climbing the stairs, he carefully removed his sandals. He paused at the door, glanced to make sure no one was around to see, and removed his outer robe, as well. He had just been in the kitchen, and that was the last to be cleansed of leaven. And...the lamb. He had cared for that filthy straw, and while he was normally fastidious about not getting the muck on himself, even the scent could contaminate the room. And as long as no one was about to see him less than fully dressed, then he would protect the cleanliness of the room with the same vigilance he used to protect the care of the lamb.

It was good to just step into the upper room. It was dark and cool for all that it was closer to the sun. The low table was set up and covered with a common cloth to keep dust off of it. Benches were already placed around it, with cushions ready so that those dining might recline in comfort like free men. Pallu checked the linens hanging on pegs by the door; they were some of the finest in the house, and had been freshly washed. They still smelled of the sweet grass which they had lain on to dry. He circled around the table, and opened the chest at the back of the room. Neatly tucked in clean wool, he was able to see the plates and cups that were kept set apart from common use. His master had a fine enough house that both sets of his dishes were decent, but these had been heirlooms for generations. Silver goblets and serving dishes of fine embossed pottery sat in that chest, ready and waiting. Pallu gently closed the lid. There would be time enough to set everything out later.

Next to the chest, Pallu lifted the lids of smaller baskets. One contained nuts, ready to set out in decorative bowls, and the other had fresh figs and dates for those at the feast to nibble on as it drew to a close. He was kneeling and so close to the baskets that the rich scent of the figs flowed out into the air towards him. It was hard work not to lift one out and have a taste now, just to make sure they were as good as they smelled. But he hadn't put so much care into each detail of this room just to take advantage of it now. The figs needed to be kept ready in their entirety. There was nothing else to do to prepare until the time came to actually set the feast out. Pallu replaced the tops of the baskets, and paused in the stillness of the waiting room. It was good to be away from everyone, and let his careful dignity relax. He constantly guarded his position as the head servant, but here he could cease worrying about how well the others followed him. His hands rested on his thighs, and he opened his palms up, letting his fingers curl gently.

"Ha Shem," he breathed into the dim air, "I have sought to do all things well, and I ask that You see my work and bring me my reward. Lift me out of my slavery as You lifted Yosef. Have favor upon me, O God, King of the Universe, and bring my time of servitude to an end…let me once again be master of myself and my own household."

Pallu felt that the room itself listened, and it was kind. He hoped that the great Lord would feel kindly to him, as well, and he stood up to head back down to the kitchen, have his meal, and check the final preparations. And hopefully that woman Ruth would be nowhere near.

Pallu had just dropped bits of stew in his beard and was working intently on cleaning them out when Meshullam walked back into the kitchen, munching on a fig. "Ah, Pallu…I was just upstairs, and it looks like nearly everything is completely ready. I'm unsure of the figs, though…are there quite enough? My brother was just here, and he is sending a servant to the market for some final things; I told him he could have use of my donkey if he brought back more figs. I saw the donkey under the tree with the blanket on already, so we shall give him what he expects, and let him have a nice trip into town, eh?"

Pallu fought down his irritation and fear. He had worked so hard to make sure that every market trip was pleasant for the donkey. If this other servant ruined his careful work, he'd have a stubborn and resistant animal to deal with. But in the face of Meshullam's confidence, what could he say? He managed to choke out a "very well...I'll go make sure the donkey has had a good drink before he is needed."

Meshullam clapped him on the back with enthusiasm. "Well done, Pallu. We can't risk being low on figs." He pulled a second fig out of his pouch as he walked away, and in his frustration Pallu forgot about the bits of stew dotting his beard. If another servant was coming to get the donkey, he wanted to make sure he was there to give exact instructions on how to coax this young animal. He grabbed a few handfuls of grain from Ruth's stores on his way out, pouring them into the pouch at his belt. She wouldn't miss those handfuls, and the donkey would be grateful for the treat. The day had become warm, so Pallu also took a moment outside the back door to pour a ladleful of water into his hand and dab it on his face. He didn't know how long it would take for that other servant to arrive, and it was nice to cool off briefly before waiting for him.

The donkey was showing some impatience when Pallu made it out to check on him. Even under the tree, the heat was getting to be a bit much for an animal with a blanket of his own fur, and a blanket of wool on top of that. Pallu felt bad for the animal, but if he took him in the stable, the donkey would then expect to be at rest with everything off.

In order to keep him ready for the other servant to come and collect him, Pallu would need to keep him where he was, but he needed to also keep him happy. The basin that sat at the base of the tree was empty, so of course the first thing to deal with was filling it with water.

Pallu patted the donkey's nose softly as he turned away, and found Ruth conveniently at the well. "Ah. Good. You are here, and since you're already drawing water, I need more for the donkey."

"Well, you can get some as soon as I'm done."

Pallu frowned. This was certainly not what he had meant. Why must this woman challenge him at every turn?

"No, you are to draw the water. And then take it to the donkey."

Ruth did not even turn around to talk to him as she filled her jar. "I am busy in the kitchen. I have too much to do to prepare for the Feast to spend more time out here drawing water for a man who can easily get it himself. Better for you to do more than just supervise, and let me get back to the vegetables."

Pallu tried to imagine Yosef drawing water, but failed. This was certainly not something Yosef would have done. He straightened his back like a great man, frowned at the woman, and repeated, "*You* are to draw the water. It is not *my* place, woman."

Ruth kept her back to him as she hefted the now-filled jar onto her hip. "Then you can be the one to explain to Meshullam why the lentils burned….unless you want to go stir them while I get water for your wonderful donkey."

Working in the kitchen would have been worse than drawing water, and Pallu was so furious at her that he could not find any words to make her obey his command. By the time he'd lost the urge to spit and sputter, she was already to the doorway of the kitchen, and he would have had to shout. Shouting would have drawn attention to the way she just flouted his authority, and he clamped his jaw shut. As long as no one was near, the only option left to him was to just draw the water himself, but he grumbled the whole time he raised the bucket out of the well. It took more time than he'd had to spare to fill the empty jar next to the well, and he was clumsy at lifting it. The water sloshed out onto his shoulder as he turned, leaving a large wet patch on his robe. He walked carefully and slowly back towards the tree, wondering how Ruth managed to just haul her jar in without making a mess of herself.

Pallu was still around the corner of the house when the other servant showed up. He heard two voices from the side of the house, and hurried a little, working to keep the rest of the water in the jar. As he rounded the corner, it was hard to either feel or act dignified while hefting his load. As soon as he was able to set it down, he drew himself up straight and tall. A young man was putting his hand on the donkey's halter, and Pallu frowned at him.

"Well, then, and are you here to use my donkey?"

The young man paused, but kept his hold of the halter. He looked at Pallu with consideration. "My master said that a young donkey would be ready and waiting under a tree, and we would be able to have use of it. I can't imagine he meant any other...? This one is haltered, and he has been fed and watered?"

"He has," started Pallu, "and he has been carefully trained so that he thinks going on a trip is a happy treat. He has not become stubbornly set against a journey to the market, and you will have to be careful to make sure you do not ruin this for him." He untied the small sack of grain from his belt. "Take this, and when he meets new people, make sure he has a small palmful for a treat. He views everyone as a friend now, and that helps."

The other servant accepted the sack with a nod of his head. "And burdens? Does he carry well--has he ever been ridden?"

Pallu frowned. "He does well with light burdens--again, palmfuls of grain make work sweet to this donkey--but he has not been ridden. I have been carefully working him up to that."

The other man seemed to want to respond to that but closed his mouth and turned his eyes to gaze thoughtfully at the donkey again. "Well, my master has said that his yoke is easy and his burden light, so this animal will do well to bear whatever is put on him."

"How much are you getting? I heard that figs were to be the bulk of your purchases today."

"I'm not always able to predict what my master is planning, but we will take good care of this good donkey. Palmfuls of grain as he meets people and as he carries parcels? We will definitely give him that."

The young man scratched behind the furry ears and the donkey snorted in approval. Maybe, thought Pallu, this wouldn't be a complete disaster. He untied the rope from the branch of the tree, and handed it off. As the other servant accepted it and wound it about his forearm, he paused with another question. "I was also told to ask after an upper room--one that might be prepared for the feast, and that my master may come and have use of...along with his disciples."

"Disciples? Is your master a rabbi? I thought your master was brother to mine? And how many disciples?" Pallu didn't know which question to ask first, and was taken aback at the idea of a nameless, wandering rabbi presuming to use that carefully cleaned and prepared room. And the donkey--was the donkey going to the right person?

The young man smiled. "I believe that my master would have me call your master a brother. The room is ready? There is my master and the twelve of us. I am not sure when we will be arriving, but I am glad to hear that all is prepared, as I was told it would be. My thanks for the use of the donkey; we will care for him well." He had that palmful of grain ready, and held it out to the willing donkey as he set a pleasant pace towards the road. Pallu was flummoxed at how that entire conversation had gone, and now he had the anticipation of thirteen visitors using the room that he had tended so carefully. Thirteen! He would need to speak with Meshullam, but even before that, Ruth must be notified so that she would not be caught unprepared.

The sun was getting low in the sky as the men arrived, but they still had enough time to have their Passover meal before it set completely. Pallu did not count them, but in watching the group he had a difficult time seeing who the master of this group actually was. Many of the men were kind and deferential to each other, and that seemed directed at one in particular more than the others, but that particular man did not carry himself as one in charge. Yosef in Egypt would have been easy to spot, and most of the Rabbis in Pallu's experience made sure that they were noticeable, so Pallu concluded that the Rabbi of this group wasn't here yet. Perhaps he would come when all else was settled, making sure that all was done for him before he arrived.

After the group had moved up the stairs, one man came back down and stood in the doorway to the kitchen, where Pallu and Ruth were scowling at each other. Pallu had asked after the readiness of the meat and had bitten into a sprig of the bitter herbs to make sure they would not bring shame on Meshullam's house, and Ruth had been offended that he would dare to question her abilities. And so this quiet man walked into a kitchen filled with both the heat of the fire and the heat of anger. He glanced between the two of them, and managed to speak without much betrayal of his own feelings.

"The room is exactly as we had hoped, and we can see the care that was put into making it ready. Is there water for washing that I can bring up?"

Pallu glanced out the window, hoping to see the boy somewhere about. It was not his place to draw water. The yard outside the kitchen was empty and still, however, and his next glance was towards Ruth. She had turned half aside to ladle lentils into a serving dish, but her face was still partly visible, and she was stone. Did he dare? After their earlier altercation, Pallu had his dignity as the head servant to protect, and he decided that this woman would simply do the woman's job and go draw water at his command. He turned back to the man, unsure of whether to speak to him as another servant or as their guest.

"Ruth will go get the water." As she straightened and fixed her stony glare on him again, he relented slightly. "I will bring it up to you in a few moments." It would be better that way, anyway, he tried to remind himself, he could act the host and ensure that Ruth would not flaunt his authority in front of their guests.

He waited by the stairs as Ruth first delivered the steaming dish of lentils and then stomped off to the well. She set the jar down by his feet with such force that some of the water splashed out and darkened his robe. "Careful, woman!" he grunted, but hesitated to say much more when he saw her face. He was not going to get the respect he was owed from her, and he did not want another scene while there were guests upstairs. So without another word, he lifted the jar and carried it upstairs.

As he pushed aside the curtain in the doorway, he was met by the one who was obviously the servant of the group. The man had taken off most of his clothes, and had wrapped one of the linen cloths around his waist in preparation for serving the others. He reached out and took the jar of water from Pallu with just a bit of a smile. "Thank you, friend." Pallu nodded his head, while lifting his eyebrows at the use of the word "friend." *He* wasn't the one half dressed.

"Will your master be needing anything else for the meal?" Pallu asked. He almost didn't care if he was rude.

The man's bit of a smile returned, a barely discernible twitching in his beard. "My master? No, my master has no need. But, friend, if you wouldn't mind waiting a moment, I'll return the jar to you."

Pallu crossed his arms and nodded. "I'll wait outside the curtain." He didn't feel like staying in the room at the bidding of a servant who didn't know his place. It felt better to hem and stew and glower freely where he wasn't observed, so he stood at the top of the stairs and watched the sun edge towards the horizon. The donkey was back under the tree, looking content. That was good. If he had had an unpleasant trip, he would have been showing his frustration. Instead, he seemed calm and almost half asleep from the late afternoon's warmth. He was tethered nicely, and that other servant had even thought to remove the blanket and drape it neatly over a nearby branch. Even though all looked so tidy, there were odd bits of green on the blanket and the ground underneath. Pallu squinted slightly, and realized he was seeing bits of fronds...had the servant also been buying greens for the wave offering for Firstfruits? It was early for that...Pallu frowned and pondered those bits of green while sounds of sloshing and murmuring filtered through the curtain.

There was a rise in a voice, and although Pallu could not catch all of the words, he could hear a bit of a protest in what was said. The response was too soft and measured to be discernible, but now Pallu's attention was drawn away from the donkey and his blanket, and he turned an ear towards the curtain, wondering what was going on with this strange group of men. That first voice continued to rise above the others, and it continued to sound like he was in disagreement with something. This time, though, there was soft laughter from the other men in the group at what he had said, and Pallu thought there was also laughter in the quieter voice, as well as laughter from the first one who spoke in protest. This group seemed to have a great deal of goodwill for each other.

Pallu imagined how nice it must feel to have a servant who would assist in the washing of hands or feet, as this group did. Perhaps someday he could train that boy to properly wash the feet of his betters. It was only great houses who had servants to spare for services like that. The Rabbi these men followed must really be someone to have a dedicated servant travel with them. Pallu wondered when this Rabbi would show up, and if it wasn't a bit strange to start the ceremonial washing before he even arrived. While he pondered, the group seemed to quiet down and one voice alone began to talk. The confidence of that voice caught Pallu's attention, and without really meaning to eavesdrop, he caught himself listening with the other men on the inside of that curtain, as though he were one of their group.

"Now that I, your lord and master, have washed your feet…."

Pallu didn't catch the rest of what was said as he tried to understand this. Was the Rabbi already here? Had he slipped in without Pallu's notice? If he were one of the group, which one of those men was the Rabbi who could command such service? And--Pallu was even more confused--did he just say he had washed their feet? The only one who looked ready to wash feet was the one who had been half-dressed. Pallu trained his ears on that voice-- did he recognize it? The man was saying something about servants and masters, and Pallu caught the idea that servants were no greater than their masters. He understood that concept. It made sense to him. Meshullam was greater than he was, but Pallu himself was certainly greater than either Ruth or the boy. There was a hierarchy and it was important to maintain it. But neither did that fit with what the man had been saying earlier...it truly sounded like the leader of the group was in there, not delayed, and that he had been acting as a servant. Pallu was shaking his head and trying to get his thoughts to sift down into order, when Ruth came up the stairs with a large serving dish. Fragrant steam clouded around her head, and her scowl was softened through it.

"Here you go, roast lamb for our guests, although why my brother is letting them use this room and eat our food I'll never understand. But take it in while it's warm so that Meshullam is not dishonored in his hospitality." She thrust the dish at Pallu, and he narrowly avoided getting some of the drippings on his robe. That would have drastically lowered his status in front of these men. Nevertheless, he decided not to waste time on reprimanding Ruth for her carelessness. He was too curious about what was going on behind that curtain, and who the master of this group was. A plate of steaming roast lamb was an excellent reason to enter the room uninvited and see what he could find out.

While both hands were needed to hold the serving dish, Pallu turned his back to the curtain and entered with another half-turn. The men were seated around the table, reclining on the cushions that had been laid out. Several of them turned pleased faces towards Pallu as they caught the scent of the roasted meat, and Pallu caught a snippet of conversation between two others who were seated close to where he stood.

"Remember how Yochanan said that he was not worthy to even untie the lace of his sandal? And now this....I don't know what to make of it. And how can having only the feet clean make the entire man clean?"

Pallu lost the other man's reply as he set the dish of lamb on the table. He tried to keep his head down while still placing it with a bit of grandeur, but he flicked his eyes around the group. Who was in the place of honor? The center seat should be reserved for the Rabbi who led this group, but Pallu didn't think it had been given to him. That other servant--the one who had been undressed to receive the water for washing--was in the place of honor. And he looked settled there, not ashamed of taking his master's seat. In fact, as Pallu attempted to observe without being noticeable, he saw the way the men turned their face toward that seat, and they did not act like anyone was out of place. All seemed well with them. Pallu kept his face as still as stone while he tried to make sense of his confusion. He bowed to the group after the platter had been set in place, and turned to the doorway. Instead of leaving this time, however, he turned back to face the table, standing ready as any servant would have done. The one who had been disrobed and served the others in the most menial way was definitely the center of their attention, and when he wiped his fingers and sat up, intending to talk, the rest of the group quieted down. He looked at the two who had been discussing sandal laces, and spoke softly.

"You know how those who are kings over the Gentiles behave, and how men in authority are treated as benefactors, and honored. Masters are always greater than their servants. Yet, you...it is to be different with you. Who would you say is greatest, the one in the position of honor at a table, or the one standing by the door, waiting for instructions on how to serve?" Pallu felt his face redden as the man briefly looked up at him. His hands, folded in readiness across his belly, tightened with the effort to not react in anger at the slight. This servant who behaved like a Rabbi looked around the group of men at the table before he continued to speak.

"You see, though, that I am among you as one who serves, although you call me 'Lord' and 'Rabbi.' It is right for you to do so, for you are correct. I am your Lord and Rabbi. And yet, I have set an example for you. As I have served you by washing your feet, so should you serve each other. Which of you is greater than me? Is there ever a servant greater than his master? If this is how I act among you, how blessed you will be if you act among yourselves in a similar manner."

The Rabbi had an odd look on his face as he paused. "I know that not all of you will be servants in the kingdom. I am not speaking to all of you, but to the ones I have chosen. And Scripture will be fulfilled."

He paused again, and this time Pallu backed his way through the curtain and out of the room. He had never heard the like. Yes, masters were always greater than their servants; that was the way it was. And greater servants were always above the lesser servants. Who was this man that was teaching those who followed him to turn that order all backwards? It would never work. Could Meshullam ever be expected to dish up stew and bring the bowl to Pallu? The thought was preposterous. And Yosef, to whom the Lord showed favor...as the Lord's favor was revealed, he became greater and greater, to the point of sitting alone at a high table. Even when his own brothers came before him, they bowed and he remained elevated. This Rabbi had to be insane.

Pallu moved away from the doorway and sat on the top of the steps, his thoughts in a muddle. He had long-cherished images of Yosef in his greatness playing across his mind, interspersed with the image of the disrobed Rabbi, kneeling on that carefully-swept floor to wipe away dust from twelve pairs of feet. Pallu's instinct was still to dismiss the image of the Rabbi as someone whose mind was flapping as loose as a curtain in the wind, but the man's face was hard to dismiss. He had seemed calm and in full control of himself when speaking, and the wry smile he had shown a few times hinted that he was aware of how others saw him. He didn't seem like an insane man.

Pallu was so lost in his own mental pictures and wonderings that he didn't hear much from the room, until the curtain was lifted and someone began to exit. He could feel his face flush red again at being caught sitting like a frog on the stairs, and the picture of the Rabbi kneeling by the bowl of water flashed in his mind again. That Rabbi was the first to emerge from the room, and smiled kindly as Pallu tried to maintain some dignity, brushing his own robes into place.

"The dinner was excellent, my friend. Please tell Ruth that the lamb was unsurpassed."

Pallu tried to think of how long the group had been in the room, and the likelihood of their completing the full Seder.

"And are you finished?" It didn't seem like they had been in there quite long enough, but then, he was stiff from sitting on that stair, and perhaps he'd lost track of time.

"There is one cup yet to drink, but I must spend time in prayer before I drain it. A walk and some time in the olive grove will be good before the last cup is poured." Pallu had no answer, so he simply bowed. The rabbi stood quietly while his followers filed out past him, and Pallu noticed one man who seemed to hesitate as he walked by. The rabbi looked at him and nodded, and said something too softly for Pallu to catch, although he thought he heard the words "go quickly." To be sure, these men weren't finished with their Seder yet, if one of them was still being given an errand. Before the rabbi turned to follow his men down the stairs, Pallu cleared his throat to get his attention.

"Shall I clear the food, or keep it for your return?"

The rabbi looked down at the bottom edge of the curtain in the doorway for a moment.

"It would be best for the food to be brought down and given to all in the house. Ruth's effort with the lamb and the vegetables deserves to be fully appreciated. It would be a shame to let it sit out and draw the flies."

Pallu nodded his head and wondered how this man knew Ruth's name, and why he chose to refer to her that way, instead of "the cook," or "the widow." This rabbi had odd ways.

The rabbi waited a moment more as the last of his followers moved down the stairs and away. "Friend, I want to thank you for your service this evening. I am finding that my appetite is not as great as I had anticipated. I had planned to eat these in a little bit, but I don't think that I'll be hungry for them after all. I wouldn't want them to go to waste. They are so good, they should be appreciated by someone." He reached into a pouch that hung at his waist and pulled out something in his fist. Pallu was still confused by his feelings at being called "friend," and didn't look at what was placed in his hand until the rabbi was halfway down the stairs.

He held three soft figs, at their peak of ripeness, sure to be sweet and perfect.

It was days later that Pallu heard what had been done to the rabbi, and it knocked the breath out of his lungs for several moments. He had not seemed the type to deserve such a thing--how could those filthy Romans justify such a torturous death for such a kind man? That quietness and calmness, and the way he had seemed so in command of himself, as well as the respect offered so freely from his followers, was not like the fear or anger or desperation that had characterized other followers of other enemies of the Roman state. It made no sense.

Pallu went out to the stable to spend some time with the donkey while he wrestled with his thoughts. He was initially frustrated to see that there were several things that needed doing. Normally he would have called the boy to come clean the pen, tidy the donkey's harness and blanket, and fetch the right kinds of food to keep the donkey happy. Today, he preferred to be alone. No one was around besides the donkey, and that gentle animal wouldn't think any less of him if he were a bit distracted. He let his shoulders drop and picked up the shovel. He wouldn't need to pay much attention to these tasks, and could let his mind wander.

In his mind he was still able to see Yosef, standing on a high dais with stern dignity as his brothers groveled before him. The image of Yosef sitting there came easily to Pallu out of long practice. For the first time, though, he also saw Yosef as alone--precarious in his height. Had he spent his whole life working to keep the favor of Pharaoh? His position may have been a sign of HaShem's favor, but it was also dependent on Pharaoh's whims. Yosef would have known how easily he could have been falsely accused and sent to rot in prison. He had experience with how hard he needed to work to gain favor in and out of prison, so that he could be free. But even then, had he ever been completely free? He had been wealthy and powerful and respected, but….the thought was disquieting to Pallu…had he been considered the slave of Pharaoh for the rest of his life? Had he needed to be careful about his service so that the power and wealth which had been given him wasn't taken away?

Now that Rabbi….the Rabbi hadn't worried about how he looked as he served. He seemed perfectly free to be on the floor…what kind of freedom allowed a master to serve and not lose authority? And before the Romans, it sounded like that Rabbi hadn't even tried to use any authority, hadn't used his devoted followers to speak up on his behalf. He just let the Romans and priests do whatever they wanted. Yosef would have never been silent before such injustices.

Pallu shook his head in consternation as he put the shovel back and straightened the blanket laying over the rail. After that, he really was done with the donkey's care, but his mind was still swirling and he decided to spend a bit more time in the sweet, dusty stable. He found the donkey's brush and began to work over the rear end of the donkey, letting his thoughts go with the rhythmic stroking. The kind animal, trained to patience and good humor, allowed Pallu to brush him several times over.

Pallu returned to his image of Yosef sitting at the high table. He could even envision the dishes on the table, perhaps a jeweled bowl of perfect, sweet figs....but now Pallu did not like to think of figs. That thought only led straight to sadness for the kind Rabbi. Better to think of how Yosef's greatness was acknowledged by the servants, carrying in the dishes of food, or his own elder brothers seated beneath him bowing and crouching before him...

And that Rabbi had crouched on the floor. As he performed the most menial of services, his followers had not taken the chance to sneer at his indignity, like anyone else might have done. The greatness of that Rabbi had not been sullied at all by his actions. Instead, love and respect for their rabbi had shone out of the eyes of the other men. How had those elder brothers looked at Yosef? Surely not with love--surely their eyes were clouded with fear and distrust.

The way the boy looked at Pallu.

He remembered the way the boy kept his face turned to hide his own anger and apprehension. It had always been a signal to Pallu that he was becoming more like Yosef, to get that type of deference. He had never been looked at with the expressions of love, admiration, and fellow-feeling the way those other men had looked at their rabbi.

Yosef, in his greatness, never even stooped to sit beside his own brothers at a meal. Pallu tried to picture Yosef in his godless Egyptian grandeur, kneeling on polished floors to untie the leather sandals of weary travelers. The image just could not be forced. The only person he could imagine stepping off of a gleaming dais and crouching before those who should rightly be lowering themselves was the Rabbi in Meshullam's upper room. He had carried himself with such perfect authority that he would have sat well on high dais, and he had obviously had full command of his disciple's respect, but he used it to care for them in the most basic way.

Pallu had long cherished the image of Yosef and tried to become like him. It had been such a comfort during his years of servitude. He had hoped to become like Yosef, finding the favor of HaShem and rising to preeminence in his master's household, being in charge of the others and thus spared the degradation of menial work. But somehow, Yosef in his greatness on a high dais suddenly seemed lower and less free than a half-dressed rabbi kneeling on a wooden floor. Pallu felt that all twelve of those disciples would have willingly acted as servants to him, instead of being served. How great would a man have to be to have his position untouched by his actions? And what kind of man, having achieved such greatness, would choose to become like...well, like someone like Pallu. Or like the boy, since Pallu wouldn't have lowered himself to wash other's feet. Slowly the vision of Yosef, standing tall and mighty and folding his arms as others brought food and drink, faded away. Pallu could no longer see him, and did not know any more how to act like him in the hopes of becoming like him.

It took a nudge from the donkey, bored with getting his hindquarters brushed over for the fourth time, to knock Pallu out of his musings. When he became more aware of his surroundings and the donkey's impatience, he was aware of something else: he no longer cherished a desire to become like Yosef.   He still enjoyed the story of the boy who became a slave and rose out of it, but it was no longer in his heart's core. When his mind turned inward, all he saw now was the image of the kneeling rabbi. He did not know what to do with this new vision, and stared at the donkey in consternation.

However, the donkey wasn't much help, so Pallu turned away and tried to decide if all was in order in the stable. He brushed his hand along the blanket that was resting neatly over a railing, and his fingers found fronds of palm leaves, now browned and easily crackled in his fingers. As he continued to pick more leaf bits out of the rough weave, the boy entered the stable. He stopped as soon as he saw Pallu, and Pallu watched as his eyes changed to a guarded expression before he lowered his head slightly to avoid eye contact. For the first time, Pallu noticed the first expression that had been on the boy's face, and he recognized the exhaustion and sadness from his own early days as a slave. He did not like being reminded of that time, and seeing it in the boy was unpleasant. He wished the boy would leave, but he stood there with his arms at his sides, waiting for either the criticism or command that was surely coming.

Pallu couldn't remember what he had most recently told the boy to do. He cleared his throat and tried to sound in command of his own faculties. "Did you finish your task?"

The boy kept his head down. "Yes, *Mar.*"

This wasn't helpful. "And….and what were you about to do now?"

"I just wanted to see if the donkey had need of anything. He's a nice donkey. I could brush him or care for his halter, or…." the boy continued to stand still. Pallu tried to imagine Yosef once more, but there was no picture in his head to help him know how to react with this boy. But suddenly his mind did see three figs resting in his own palm, placed there by the Rabbi. He sucked in air, filling his lungs and hoping to get some direction. He felt half-witted.

"He *is* a nice donkey, and he listens well. I have brushed his hindquarters already, but perhaps his front end could still use some attention. Has he let you approach his shoulders?"

The boy kept his head down, but slanted his eyes sideways at Pallu. This was not what he was expecting, and he didn't know how or even if he should respond. "Yes, *Mar,* several times. He likes being brushed."

Pallu saw those figs again as he extended his own hand. "Here is the brush, boy. Take good care, and remember that he listens well. You can tell him all manner of secrets."

Pallu left as the boy first looked at the brush in his hands and then at Pallu himself. As he passed through the doorway, he turned his head and caught the guarded bit of hope rising in the boy's eyes. He nodded his head slightly, and continued on towards the house.

He had hoped to go sit in the quiet of the kitchen. It was Ruth's day to do the washing, and normally the kitchen would be a place of peace without her presence. He could enjoy the smell of the herbs she stored there or have a nibble of some bread without being challenged. However, as he approached the doorway, he saw her movement within. If she had seen him, it was too late to change direction and still have dignity, but he still checked his steps in consternation. There was so much swirling about his head that he didn't feel quite up to an encounter with the master's widowed sister. And yet…due to old habits, he straightened his back and set his shoulders. He still was the greater of the servants of this house, and he must act like it.….

Again, his image of Yosef failed him. It had been so instructive for so long, but now he could only see the Rabbi on the floor. Up in that room, on the greatest night of the year, the greatest in the group of men had acted like the least. And he had instructed his followers to continue in that example. Pallu took a few more halting steps to the doorway, but his approach was nearly silent in his hesitation, and he was able to see Ruth without being noticed. She had her back to the doorway, and was working at the table, cutting vegetables. She muttered quietly and Pallu could not catch the words, but it was obvious that she was angry. While he watched, she put the knife down and made a fist, pounding hard onto the table. The knife jumped and clattered to the floor, but Ruth ignored it and stood with both palms pressing against the edge of the table. She became as still as stone.

Pallu dropped his shoulders. What good would being lord over this woman do? He had tried to protect himself by ensuring he was respected, but what was he protecting himself from? This woman's grief and rage at her own life? The one man who had seemed truly great had not shielded himself from dishonor, but had used his greatness to choose to serve. He had chosen to act as one lower than Pallu, and Pallu realized that he wanted to be as great as the kindness in that man. If one chose to serve, perhaps it did not mean one was less, maybe it meant that one had greater freedom simply to be able to have that choice. True slaves could not risk it.

Ruth heaved a huge sigh, and began to bend to finally pick up her knife. Pallu knew she would see him as she turned, and he took a step into the kitchen. "Ruth, I…." The words caught in his throat. He had to swallow to make room for them to come out properly.

"May I draw some water for you?"

UNDERSTAND

The wagon and its varied cargo had left a little bit before sunup. As soon as the guards could see well enough to drive and protect it, they had hitched up the horses and rolled away from the inn, so that Bebagin could finish out his sleep and have the leisurely breakfast that he was accustomed to. He preferred to leave at a more reasonable hour. The wagon would rumble ahead all day, and then stop an hour before sundown so that the soldiers could set up Bebagin's tent. He knew he might arrive before his tent was completely ready for him, as his chariot was so much faster. Thus, he allowed himself to linger over the inn's fine breakfast. He did not want to catch up to the wagon too early--it made him feel guilty to see the men working so hard with his tent. Besides, he had no need to worry--all was well prepared and in motion, and it may be some time before he was able to enjoy such soft, fresh bread again. The inn he had chosen was excellent, but it had not served up good bread like this for the past week. There had been baskets of hard, flat stuff that the Hebrew innkeeper said was part of his religious observances. Bebagin had had to send Mahdi out to find a Roman woman with a stall of good bread, and smuggle it up to his rooms without the innkeeper's notice. But now, the morning he was leaving, apparently the religious observation was at an end and there was good bread once more at his table. He chose to take his time enjoying it.

However, he may have lingered a bit too long this time, as he noticed Mahdi standing in the doorway--and not just standing, but shifting his weight from foot to foot in an attempt at respectful patience. "Ah, Mahdi, are we ready? Is your work finished, and now it is time to get underway?"

Mahdi stilled his feet and kept his gaze low. "Overseer, the horses are stamping their hooves at the door."

Bebagin glanced at the basket still half full of warm bread. "As are you, Mahdi, as are you. Well, it does not do to keep restless horses waiting, and I know you understand those horses better than anyone." It was why he had specifically asked Candace Amanitore for Mahdi as his chariot driver. She had barely paused before granting his request. Bebagin usually got what he requested of her, even though getting her to agree to this trip at all had taken a little more convincing than usual. Once he had gotten approval for his journey, though, it was all more a matter of notifying her what resources he would need. And Mahdi, with his famous driving ability, was one of those resources. The fact that the Candace had barely paused--even if just barely--was a testament to how Mahdi's reputation was known even before her throne. Mahdi was worth listening to when he said the horses were getting impatient.

"If all is ready, I will be there momentarily." Mahdi nodded his bald head and turned to leave. In true Egyptian fashion, he shaved his head carefully, and wore a linen headscarf to keep cool when he was either outside or in formal situations. Bebagin never understood why he also chose to shave off his eyebrows with the rest of his hair. Well, Mahdi was nearly as good as a magician with those horses, and there was no accounting for the oddities of magicians. Whether or not he had eyebrows did not change his excellence as a chariot driver.

Bebagin stood as he reached for one last small loaf. There would already be sacks of dried figs and salted fish in the chariot for their mid-day meal, but now that this inn had real bread, and it was almost as good as the bread at home, he would enjoy one last loaf greatly as he set out on his journey. It was with a sigh that he turned away from that nicely provisioned table, to be met by the innkeeper at the door.

These Hebrews never quite knew how to treat those of rank. Years of exile and occupation had made it so they weren't proud, exactly, but you would think they wouldn't evidence quite such independence after being ruled for so many centuries. At home, Bebagin was usually met with lowered heads as people crouched on the floor. He knew that when Mahdi had been shifting his feet, it was partly in impatience, and partly in the impulse to sink to the floor as he addressed the Overseer of the Queen's Treasuries. This Hebrew simply stood.

"I wanted to thank you for your presence at my inn, and give you my wishes for a pleasant journey back to your own country. I hope to see you again someday."

Bebagin tilted his head slightly as he regarded this innkeeper. "It was fascinating to see your Temple, and an honor to learn of your God. Even if I was not allowed in the inner courts, it was greatly interesting. I may be back….I would like to participate in your Feasts *after* the harvest."

The Hebrew paused and seemed to check what he wanted to say. Instead of replying to Bebagin's idea of worshipping at the Temple again, he chose a safer route and asked "Do you have all of the provisions that you need for your journey?"

Bebagin smiled. He, too, would keep to safer subjects. "I do, and I give you thanks. I have enjoyed your bread very much, and am actually taking a loaf with me, if that is acceptable to you."

The innkeeper nodded, and responded, "If you would like more, *Mar*, I would be happy to get some wrapped for you."

"I believe that what I have is enough." Bebagin couldn't resist poking at this Hebrew a little. "I will enjoy it while I read. I picked up a scroll of one of your prophets….Ysha`yahu, I believe? I am looking forward to learning more of your religion and your nation's past."

The innkeeper stood with his mouth open for a moment. "You….are reading the prophet? You went to the Temple, and now you are reading Yesha`yahu?

Bebagin faked confusion. "Does that cause you consternation? Surely your god would accept worship from any who wanted to give it? Doesn't every god desire greater glory?"

The innkeeper opened his mouth and closed it several more times. Whatever he actually wanted to say was swallowed down as he kept to more prudent paths. "The Torah says there is to be but one law amongst Hebrew and foreigner, and if you choose to follow that law, you cannot be anything but welcome. May blessings be on your travels."

Bebagin smiled and nodded again, and decided not to push the upright dignity of this man any longer, but swept out of the inn and to the courtyard. After briefly patting the muzzles of the horses and touching his own forehead in respect to the work they were about to engage in, he stepped up into his chariot. Mahdi was carefully keeping his eyes over the backs of the horses, but still respectfully lowered his head. "Are you ready, Overseer?" he asked, trying to not sound impatient.

"Do we have everything, Mahdi?"

"Everything that was not loaded in the wagon, Overseer."

"The bags of figs and pistachios?"

"Yes…."

"And what of the chest of idols?"

"Under your seat, Overseer, and your scrolls are also in the chest."

"Very good. It will be pleasant to practice my Hebrew and keep occupied while we drive. Let's begin."

It was early enough in the year that the roads weren't completely dust, and Mahdi knew just the right speed to drive the horses so that they kept ahead of what dust they did end up sifting into the air behind them. For some time, Bebagin enjoyed watching the city as they trotted along. It may be quite a number of years before he journeyed up north this far again. Israel had some good things to offer; nuts and olive oil and wool, if one were so disposed to such cloth, but Rome had more and was easier to get to. Candace Amanitore really had needed some stiff persuasion to agree to this journey of Bebagin's, and had held her doubts as to whether wool were worth allowing her trusted Overseer of the Treasury to engage on a several-month journey. But Bebagin had not become Overseer through a lack of personal abilities, and he knew how to be persuasive.

Once he tired of watching the city of Jerusalem dwindle away behind them, and the countryside became monotonous and boring once more, Bebagin reached under his seat and pulled the small trunk towards his feet. His iron keys to the many different chests traveling home with him were on a loop on his belt, hidden in the folds of his robe. Although the chest by his feet was the smallest of all treasure-laden boxes, the key was of a size with the others, and it took him a moment to sort through and find the correct one. It was a pleasure, though, to turn it in the lock and open the chest. The wagon ahead contained things that would enrich the Candace's treasury, but these were his own bits of treasure.

Bebagin smiled as he lifted up the first layer of wool. The first face he saw was that of Bes. He had come looking for new gods and new stories to believe in, but seeing the familiar squat shape of the little deity, one that had surely traveled all the way from home to this far-off place, had melted his heart. He poked the protuberant belly. "I have no prayers to make for children of my own, Bes, but perhaps you can find ways to smile upon me as I return you to our homeland? Keep accidents away from us, maybe?"

Beneath Bes was more wool, and tucked deep inside were three Roman *Lares*, beautiful figures of bronze. They were so detailed, especially next to old Bes, and seemed more delicate than their poured metal figures really were. He lifted out the one on the right, his *Lares Viales*, holding a whip in one hand and a scroll--presumably a map--in the other. Bebagin turned this *Lares* about in his hand a few times, admiring the fine workmanship.

"Well, here you are on a journey. This should be familiar to you, O god of roads. If you give me safe--and swift--movement towards my home, I will give you a fig at every cairn I find along the way."

Mahdi barely turned his head towards his shoulder, but Bebagin noticed the movement. "Do you object, Mahdi?"

"No, Overseer, certainly not. I am only wondering if we have enough figs. There are many cairns along this road for that type of Roman god."

"We can always buy more figs if we run out, Mahdi." He could tell by the set of the driver's shoulders that this was still not a satisfactory answer. Mahdi liked figs. Bebagin smiled a little. "Giving up our own figs will be a small sacrifice if it keeps bandits and wild animals and rain away. A good, safe, dry road that we can run along quickly? That is worth letting go of our own figs, is it not?"

Mahdi still worked to maintain his posture. "If the god were real and heard you, and was disposed to honor your requests, Overseer, then yes. But perhaps offerings and prayers to Khonsu, the traveler with the moon, would be better for you to petition?"

"Perhaps Khonsu is still in Egypt and too far away to hear us, Mahdi, and this *Lares Viales* is closer and more effective?"

"Perhaps." But Mahdi was still holding a firm posture to not let any of his own emotions show through. Bebagin smiled at his back, then replaced the *Lares Viales*. He lifted another bit of wool to look at the *Lares Augustus* and the *Lares Patrii.* He had been so drawn to the *Lares Familii*, with his kind smile and fatherly air, but not being able to have children of his own made that one seem inappropriate. What if he had gotten the *Lares Familii*, and the god had been frustrated by not having a household and family to work with? He might have caused mischief in Bebagin's own life, and that was not something Bebagin needed. Candace Amanitore did enough of that on her own. So, he had set down the kind-looking god with a shrug, and picked up the *Lares Patrii.* This one looked much sterner, an expression he remembered on his own father's face long ago before he had been chosen for the palace.

Even as he had been ushered into the wagon with other boys who had also been chosen, and they all knew they were destined to serve within the crowd of eunuchs, his father had had that stern expression. There was no pride in his son's rise to position, no grief at the loss of the continued family line, no kind wishes for what was to happen to Bebagin or for his recovery. There was just sternness. This *Lares Patrii* might be of the same material as his father, and even if the god spoke Latin, perhaps he could convince that Egyptian man in his Egyptian underworld to feel kindly now.

Mahdi once again turned his head to barely glance over his shoulder. "Did you hear the stories of the land, Overseer?"

Bebagin grinned broadly at that. Mahdi may not approve of giving up figs, but he enjoyed the stories as much as anyone else.

"Well, the Roman ones we know. I purchased the *Lares* because they were beautiful, not to learn more Roman stories. Worshiping at the Hebrew Temple, however...there were many stories, and it was interesting to hear them from the Hebrew perspective. You might not remember some of the stories of when Egypt ruled the world and the Hebrews were their slaves...do you?"

Mahdi turned his head fully this time. If his eyebrows hadn't been shaved off, they would have climbed high on his forehead. "I...may have heard hints of that while we stayed here, Overseer. But never at home."

Bebagin chuckled. "No pharaoh wants to keep a record of shame. Those stories were destined to be buried. I found the steles deep in the back of storage rooms, and there is no telling how old they are. There are edicts against the Hebrews; apparently they were making bricks but also starting to get a bit insolent and defiant. And close to a few of those, I found the clay tablets from various tributaries asking the pharaoh for help defending against the Hebrews, after they had left Egypt. One hinted--and not very subtly, I cannot imagine any Pharaoh taking kindly to the insults-- about a great loss of both wealth and children that the Egyptians had suffered."

"Children?"

Ah, he had Mahdi now. This story was too fascinating. Bebagin may have the official title of Overseer of the Treasury, but he was a gifted storyteller and well known at the palace for the tales that he collected every time he could convince Candace Amanitore to let him go on a diplomatic trip. He had gathered a wealth of tales as great as the wealth of goods.

"Well, this is where visiting the Hebrew temple during their holy days had great value. The steles and tablets stored in the palace do not give much information, but this was a great victory for the Hebrews, and the center of the celebration I came for. You see, they had a great magician who demanded the release of the Hebrews, but of course no Pharaoh would willingly let go of slaves who were building his monument. But that magician, he was able to turn the mighty Nile into blood."

Mahdi gasped and turned his head again, this time pulling on the reigns and misdirecting the horses. The chariot wobbled and Bebagin nearly lost his grip on the *Lares Patrii*. Dropping the god into the dust of the road would not earn him any favors from either the deity or his father. "Careful, Mahdi….I won't tell you the story if you cannot listen and drive well."

Mahdi kept himself facing forward this time, but he bent his knees slightly and lowered his head. "I beg your forgiveness, Overseer. Did the Nile really become blood?"

"Oh, that long distant past, who is to tell? If it did, no stele in any storage room will admit to it. But it is what the Hebrews firmly believe. Beyond that, they have tales of frogs and locusts overrunning the land, a time when the magician threw ash into the air and it became boils on all the people, and when he was even able to make the sun itself go dark….hmm."

Bebagin was silent for many seconds, watching the road flow away beneath the wheels of the chariot. Mahdi did not dare risk looking back at him, but after such a pause, he did manage a respectful "Overseer?"

Bebagin shook his head and shrugged his shoulders. "Ah, it was small but interesting. As part of the celebration last week, the Hebrews recited the evils brought upon the Egyptians by this magician. When they got to the one about the sun going dark, many of them became quiet. You could hear the shuffling of their feet louder than their voices. Something about that one unsettled them, even though it was a great feat of their own magician."

Bebagin paused again while Mahdi expertly guided the horses around a great divot in the road. "Well done, Mahdi. See? Bess is helping you avoid mishap. Or maybe the *Lares Viali.* Those figs will be well earned." Mahdi chose not to respond, and Bebagin grinned at his back once more.

"At any rate, according to the Hebrew stories, the final act of the magician was to summon his god to kill every firstborn, whether man or animal. Pharaoh's own son, protected in the heart of his palace, was even found dead. But the Hebrews were spared. They had sacrificed lambs and painted the blood on their doorposts, and were kept safe. The next morning, Egypt vomited them out of her land, chasing them away with gold and jewelry. They couldn't get rid of the Hebrews quickly enough, it seems. And that was the point of their celebration at their temple. They recited the woes brought upon the Egyptians, and sacrificed lambs to eat at home with their families. There was great singing, and such crowds with so many lambs....and such a flow of blood coming out of their temple. It was a river of blood. The Hebrews were joyous in their celebration of being free people--but a few also cried out prayers for deliverance from Romans. Those were shushed quickly, however, with many side glances at any who seemed an outsider. The Roman guards walking about didn't seem to care about the occasional complaint as long as no one drew a sword, though. And I? Well, they may look askance at me, but eunuchs aren't allowed in their temple, and I have no desire to stir up a political mess. I just wanted to observe as much as I could and not cause a problem."

Mahdi had been paying such close attention to the story that he hadn't noticed the cairn coming up on the side of the road. Bebagin used the head of the *Lares Patrii* to poke him in the back. "Slow down, Mahdi, stop at the cairn and let us see who it is dedicated to." Mahdi had to pull hard on the horses to get them to slow and stop, and when they had, they stomped their hooves in disapproval. Bebagin tucked the *Lares* back into the wool in the chest before he gathered his robes about him and stepped down. "Shall we practice our Latin, Mahdi? Listen: *Larius Viabilus*....well, that's good enough. We know to leave a fig here. Hand me the sack, will you, Mahdi?"

Mahdi pretended to have to search for it, taking his time opening other sacks first. Bebagin fought his grin down and chose to find the stern face he had seen so much on his own father. "It's no use, Mahdi. The sack is by your feet, and I am aware that you've already had more than one fig. Hand it over." Mahdi paused, his face turned away, then slowly lifted the sack and extended his arm toward Bebagin. It was not as full as it had been when they started out.

"Hmm....we don't wish to offend this god. Since some of these figs have already been enjoyed, perhaps we should leave two for the god. Or three?" He pretended not to notice the widening of Mahdi's eyes. "Well, maybe two will be generous enough. A smooth road, clear weather, and no rascals to harass us. That is worth two figs." He set them in the dust at the base of the cairn. Once they were dirty like that, few would come and try to eat them, so it was a good way to dedicate them to whatever *Lares* might be listening. He made no bow, but simply inclined his head slightly. The Overseer of the Candace's treasury was too great to bow to a nameless, foreign, minor deity, but he felt that his offering of friendship should be enough to get some favor.

It was with his dignity intact that he again gathered his robes to keep them out of the dust, and stepped back up into his chariot. As he settled into his seat, he glanced at the chest holding his own bits of treasure from this land. "Well, Mahdi, drive on, but be sure to stop at the next cairn. We have many more figs to offer. Meanwhile, I believe I will pull out one of the Hebrew scrolls, and perhaps learn their stories more. It is always good to have stories to share."

He balanced the scroll on his lap while he closed the chest and locked it. When it had been safely tucked under his seat again, he unrolled the scroll some ways and picked a place at random.

"'Awake, awake, put on your strength, Tziyon; put on your beautiful garments, Yerushalayim, the holy city: for henceforth there shall no more come into you the uncircumcised and the unclean....' Well, Mahdi, that is not the case for Jerusalem yet. *I* was allowed into the city. Uncircumcised? Perhaps we shall not discuss that." Mahdi kept himself focused on the road. He also was a eunuch; in fact, the entirety of the Candace's household was. The next Pharaoh's bloodline must be protected, after all. It was an honor to serve the Candace, but it did mean an ongoing sadness at the loss each man had suffered to do so. It was not a comfortable thing to discuss, and interesting that this Hebrew God would choose to keep him away.

"Let's look for something more welcoming from the Hebrew God. Or maybe he is all condemnation and wishes to keep such as we are away?" Bebagin moved one long finger down the careful writing, moving slowly as he translated the text in his head. "Ah, listen to this, it's far more comforting: ' Therefore my people shall know my name: therefore they shall know in that day that I am he who does speak; behold, it is I….How beautiful on the mountains are the feet of him who brings good news, who publishes shalom, who brings good news of good, who publishes salvation, who says to Tziyon, Your God reigns!' Think of that, Mahdi….if we were to bring to the Candace news that her gods ruled supreme and were in her favor, if we brought news of victory and peace...would she think our feet were beautiful?"

Mahdi kept his face properly forward this time, but he shrugged his shoulders. "It would be difficult for her to see our feet, Overseer, if we were bowing before her."

"True, that is true. When lowering oneself down, one's robes do tend to cover one's feet."

Mahdi had no response to that. His position did not warrant the long flowing robes that Bebagin wore with such dignity. As a chariot driver and one who cared for horses, his robes were shorter and more utilitarian.

"Well, Mahdi, let us continue, whether or not our feet will be declared beautiful. We will not likely have such good news as this prophet mentions, at any rate." He looked down at the scroll, and the spot where his finger rested. 'Behold, my servant shall deal wisely, he shall be exalted and lifted up, and shall be very high.' It is nice for a servant to be lifted up, is it not, Mahdi? Perhaps, if you are wise, you will become great someday, also. I wonder if this is the prophet's servant, or a servant of the god?

"'Like as many were astonished at you (his visage was so marred more than any man, and his form more than the sons of men)'…Mahdi, this does not sound like a servant who was actually lifted up. A marred visage and form? That is someone returning from war….or from the prison, to be honest. Not one who was honored….perhaps we shall gain more understanding from continuing, hmm?

"'so shall he sprinkle many nations; kings shall shut their mouths at him: for that which had not been told them shall they see; and that which they had not heard shall they understand.' This is quite the promise! Mahdi, if I did not tell you something, would you be expected to understand? You did not even see the cairn until I pointed it out. With all of that talk of beautiful feet and good news, I was expecting something a little easier to understand. Great victory, certain rule, but here kings are getting their mouths shut. Candace Amanitore shuts her mouth often…but it's usually a sign that she is done listening to some poor groveler."

Mahdi grunted. It was a good thing he couldn't see Bebagin grinning at his back. "What was that?" Bebagin poked him, this time with his finger. "Did you have something you were thinking about our Candace?"

"No, Overseer." It was the only answer the poor man could make safely, but Bebagin decided to poke him again.

"Had you groveled before the Candace with a request, and had her mouth closed to you?"

Mahdi did not respond, but only continued to focus down the road, driving the horses at their pleasant trot. He really was an excellent driver, gently curving around bumps or holes in the road that might be jarring, and he knew a pace that kept the horses happy. He'd always had quite the reputation for covering the longest distances in a day, due to not pushing the animals too hard, and their stamina lasted longer. He also was known for driving the chariot carefully, and rarely needing repairs. Those who drove with less care tended to have chariots that broke down more frequently, as well as injured and unhappy horses. So Bebagin had gotten the best, and he did drive well, but sometimes one wondered if the man actually dared to have opinions. Bebagin folded the scroll slightly and poked the back of Mahdi yet again.

"Well, did you?"

"Only before this journey, Overseer."

"Well, you couldn't have had the opportunity once we'd left on this trip. So, what was your request that the Candace shut her mouth to?"

Mahdi was silent and still except for slight movements of his wrists as he sent subtle messages to the horses. Bebagin was enjoying his discomfiture hugely. He worked hard to keep his face and his voice stern. "Are you not going to answer me? Is it your right to shut *your* mouth?"

He couldn't even see the muscles in the man's face move as he grunted "I asked her to spare me from having to go on this journey."

Bebagin chose to be amused instead of offended, and laughed loudly, smacking the man on his back and causing him to lurch forward over the rail of the chariot. The horses were momentarily confused and faltered in their steps before Mahdi sent reassurance and direction to them again. Bebagin continued to chuckle.

"And well, here we are. Has it not been a pleasant journey? Have you not seen interesting sights, and been well fed? Are you not glad of the diversion in your otherwise mundane life?"

"I am grateful for my life in Egypt, Overseer. I enjoy your stories from your travels very much, but none of them has ever made me long to see the lands they are from. As far as journeys go, this one has been much better than most, and I am glad now that I came. But before we left, it seemed a hard thing to me…." Mahdi didn't want to risk looking back at Bebagin to see how well he was taking this moment of candor, nor did he want to continue and risk punishment for contrary thoughts. Bebagin finished his sentence for him.

"And you thought you'd rather stay in civilized Egypt? I understand. It is certainly still the best of all countries, no matter how well the Roman army is able to conquer the rest of the world. And yet, it is delightful to know the other gods and their tales. The best way to discover that is to go myself, and the Candace will never object as long as I prove that it is also a way to enrich her treasury. And somewhere, I am sure, there is a tale of a god that will be the best of all tales. I love Egypt and her stories, but maybe I've gotten used to them. They have paled over time. New stories help, and I feel like I'm hearing whispers of better ones yet with each new tale that I encounter. Perhaps even in this scroll that better tale is hiding. I will stop poking you, perhaps, and read more?"

Mahdi's shoulders dropped a nearly indiscernible amount in relief. Bebagin had been watching him carefully, or he wouldn't have quite caught it. Yes, he had probably poked Mahdi quite enough. It would not be to the good of the horses or the ease of the road to get Mahdi too uptight. His best decision now would be to let the man alone, so he turned back to the scroll. "Where were we? I lost my place, talking about the mouths of rulers getting shut." He moved his finger along the column of writing. "Let's start here: 'Surely he has borne our sickness, and carried our suffering; yet we considered him plagued, struck by God, and afflicted.' This sounds terrible. And none of it is clear, is it? Of course, if a prophet spoke in an intelligible manner, then he could be proven wrong more easily and would lose his status as prophet. Have you been able to listen much to the Candace's most honored prophets? They rarely say anything that does not sound like gibberish; 'the full moon will bring forth newness,' and such nonsense. They can't be proven wrong, so they can't lose their position.

"Yet, it is quite the thought, is it not? That someone might bear our suffering? That someone else might be considered afflicted in our place? I will say to only you, Mahdi, that while it is a great honor to serve in the Candace's household, I do wish it hadn't come at such a price. What legacy can I leave to carry on my name? When Bebagin crosses the river to the underworld, who will remember him? Who will ensure that my burial rites are performed, and that I will have what I need to be well in the afterlife? Perhaps, if I am exceptionally good at serving Candace Amanitore, she will make sure that I have at least a coin under my tongue to pay the dark ferryman and a few goods to make me comfortable. But no one will be left to remember my name, to tell my stories…except perhaps other eunuchs like you, Mahdi. You are so young, it is likely that you will be around to speak my name and keep my memory for a little while. Will you do that for Bebagin?"

Mahdi did not hesitate this time. "Oh, yes, Overseer."

"Yes, we eunuchs must be fathers and sons to each other, must we not? But who will speak your name after you cross the river, Mahdi?"

"I do not know, Overseer."

"It is a sadness, Mahdi, a great sadness that we might not ever cease to mourn. We must find our joy in serving our Candace. However great this man is of whom the Hebrew prophet speaks, there is none who can take this sadness from us and carry it himself. Even if there were a prophet who was willing to become a eunuch in our place, it cannot undo what was done." Mahdi shifted his feet slightly. "I know, Mahdi, it is not a nice thing to remember. Forgive me for dwelling on it. I will keep reading.

"'He was oppressed, yet when he was afflicted he didn't open his mouth; as a lamb that is led to the slaughter, and as a sheep that before its shearers is mute, so he didn't open his mouth. By oppression and judgment he was taken away; and as for his generation, who among them considered that he was cut off out of the land of the living for the disobedience of my people to whom the stroke was due?''

Bebagin thought back to the Hebrew temple during those great holy days, and the lambs that each family had brought. Those lambs had been quiet. This prophet, meanwhile, had a lot to say. The idea of one who would even attempt to bear another's suffering, but do it silently, had Bebagin finally run out of words himself. He was quiet as Mahdi slowed down the horses to match the pace of a wagon in front of them. This part of the road was a bit busier, and Bebagin knew that Mahdi regretted having to adjust his own excellent driving to not crash into others. In Egypt, the great chariots were recognized, and all others moved aside. Here, he was just one of many, and it was Mahdi who had to adapt. Fortunately, most of those on foot at least knew enough to keep well away from the wheels of a good chariot like his. Bebagin spent a few more moments watching some of the people that they passed. He was so uncharacteristically quiet, and for so long, that finally Mahdi risked looking back over his shoulder. The horses were moving slowly enough now that the risk was well calculated and his movement did not translate to signals along the reigns.

"Overseer? Are you well?"

Bebagin laughed and decided to poke Mahdi's back once more. "Too quiet, am I? You don't quite know what to do with Bebagin if he is silent, eh? Well, Mahdi, I am merely wandering in the confusion of my own head. I had hoped to find more stories to add to my collection, stories that brought the joy I used to have in our Egyptian ones, but this one has me more confused. The stories of the Romans are intelligible, and if they are not beautiful, they are at least entertaining. This Hebrew prophet, however, I do not understand his story at all. This is more exact than what the

Candace's prophets utter regarding newness and moons, but it is also quite confusing."

It seemed perfectly natural for the man walking closest to the chariot to simply ask "Do you not understand what you are reading?"

Also naturally, Bebagin simply responded. "I understand the words, but not who the prophet is talking about. Is it himself? Many prophets like to ensure their own greatness through their prophecies. Or is he serving someone else and trying to make that one greater?"

Then Bebagin looked at the strange man. He was breathing a little heavily as if he had been running, but otherwise he seemed completely at ease while walking beside the chariot of a great man, interrupting a private conversation. Bebagin poked Mahdi in the back. "Stop."

The horses paused, nodding their heads and snorting slightly, as the chariot rested in the dust in the middle of the road. They were cursed roundly in Latin as a mere farm wagon had to swerve sharply to avoid hitting them, then the wagon driver was cursed as those on foot had to avoid getting hit themselves. In the midst of all that cursing and chaos, Bebagin tipped his head to consider the man who had also stopped, standing by the chariot as if he belonged there. "You are bold. I am not usually spoken to as I pass by other men."

The man continued to stand. He did not bow before Bebagin, he did not even lower his head. He had to lift his chin slightly to look into Bebagin's face, which he did without shame. He even narrowed his eyes slightly as if he were considering how well he liked the man in rich robes who was seated in the fine chariot. His head was as bald as Mahdi's, but he had his own eyebrows and a large beard. Bebagin had wondered at the Hebrew custom of growing such beards, and realized that this man must also belong to that people.

"You are a Hebrew?" The man nodded. Bebagin chose to be pleased and smiled greatly at him. "Well, you may be exactly the teacher that Mahdi and I need. We are trying to understand the writings of one of your prophets, but it simply does not make sense. Explain this to me, and tell me who the prophet is talking about?" He extended the scroll slightly towards the bearded man and tapped the section he had just read.

There was the hint of a smile deep inside that beard. "This is Messiah Yeshua, the Savior of the world."

Bebagin considered those titles for a moment. "These are not stories that I have heard. Is that tale farther along in the scroll?"

The man shook his head. "This prophet only foretold of the Messiah. The stories of what he did during his life are still being written down. I do not have a scroll about him, but I walked alongside him for three years, and I can tell you myself."

Bebagin considered the bearded Hebrew for another moment before laughing and slapping the partially rolled parchment against his thigh. He poked Mahdi once more. "Do you hear that, Mahdi? Instead of reading the scroll of a long-dead prophet, we have the chance to hear new stories from a living man, himself! Shall we listen?"

Mahdi had his shoulders a little hunched but he responded quietly "It may be interesting, Overseer."

Bebagin waved a hand at the man. "Well, where are you going? Do our paths point in the same direction? Would you like to rest your feet and ride with me while you tell me more of this Messiah Yeshua? I am Bebagin, Overseer of the Treasury of the Candace in Ethiopia, but I am also a collector of tales and a man who delights in what is curious. If your own travels are down this road, perhaps we can travel together."

The man's eyes were calm as he responded "I was only told to come here, and I would be glad of the chance to tell you of my Lord."

"You were told? Will your master, then, be angry with you for running off? I have no desire to either harbor a misbehaving servant, or deal with an angry master."

There was a definite smile now, easy to see as the man's entire beard shifted. "I am doing exactly what my master wishes. I will ride with you."

Bebagin pulled the little chest containing the *Lares* and old Bes from under his seat and settled it closer to Mahdi's feet. Mahdi glanced down slightly and shifted his weight as the man stepped up. Bebagin pointed at the chest and told him "Be seated there. Mahdi will not poke you, and I want to see your face as you tell me this story. The more I watch and listen, the better I will be able to retell it at home."

The man sat down and rested his hands in his lap. He seemed quite sure of himself. His robes weren't anything worth noticing, and he carried no bag, nor did he have attendants. Bebagin was sure that he was simply a common man, and yet he seemed completely at ease speaking to the Overseer of the Candace's Treasury as an equal. Bebagin was nearly as curious about the man himself as he was about the explanation of the inscrutable prophet. Since the man seemed to be waiting for Bebagin to ask questions, Bebagin decided to do just that.

"Well, and what is your name? If we are going to talk, tell me who you are."

"My name is Pilipos."

"Just that? No 'Pilipos of somewhere?' No 'Pilipos belonging to the house of anyone?'"

"Just Pilipos, a son of God and disciple of the Son of Man, the Light of the world, the Savior of all men."

"Ah, those are great titles. You are the son of a god?"

"I am a son of *the* God, brought into his family through the adoption made possible by the sacrifice of His own Son, my Rabbi, Messiah Yeshua, who came to be the sacrificial lamb that takes away the sins of men and grants us our adoption into the family of God."

Bebagin was glad to finally have something recognizable. "Ah, sacrificial lamb! That is what your prophet said--one would be led like a lamb to the slaughter. Was your rabbi killed, then?"

"He was crucified by the Romans on the night of Passover two years ago. They had no charge against him, yet they killed him, and after three days he lived again. I had breakfast with him along the shore of the Sea of Tiberias."

"He died and then lived again? Excellent. Did you know that the god of the underworld, Osiris, also died and then lived?"

"I am not familiar with the Egyptian gods."

"No, you would not be, would you? The Hebrews are notorious for their single-mindedness. I was intrigued to learn that, due to that notoriety, you are the only people group that Caesar exempts from required worship in his temples. Well, tell me more of this Rabbi. You called him 'The Son of Man.' Aren't all men the son of some man or another?"

Pilipos pointed at the scroll that was still held loosely in Bebagin's hands. "At the beginning of his writings, the prophet says that 'the Lord himself will give you a sign: behold, a virgin shall conceive, and bear a son, and shall call his name Immanu'el.' My Rabbi was born of a virgin, and the very heavens testified to that fact. He is God himself, but born into mankind. Therefore, he is God as the Son of Man."

Bebagin was loving this story. "Born of a virgin, hmm? That is a nice idea. How, exactly, did the heavens testify of that?"

"A great star appeared over his birth place, and the very heavens were opened to reveal angels singing for the joy of his birth."

Bebagin was quiet as he thought for just a moment. "How long ago was your Rabbi born?"

"Thirty-five years."

This did get Bebagin to pause. For the first time that day, he felt himself frowning a bit. "I seem to remember hearing of a great star that only appeared for a time. The prophets at the Candace's palace prophesied that it meant new and glorious things for our queen. They kept it vague, of course. She hoped it meant victory over the Romans, but knew it could also mean a more beautiful piece of silk from the east. You mean that it was on account of your Rabbi's birth? Did any other great and wonderful signs attest to his divinity?"

"Yes, many. Too many to relate them all. There was a crowd of angels at Messiah Yeshua's birth--like the heavens cracked open and spilled out glory. The shepherds who witnessed it still can't talk intelligibly about it."

"Are shepherds ever intelligible? But in spite of stupid shepherds, this has the makings of a great story. This is a good beginning, a very good beginning, and it will be excellent to hear more! What other signs?"

"Healing, teaching, feeding. He shut the mouths of the Pharisees more than once."

Bebagin laughed and sat up straight and slapped his leg."Ha! *He* shut *their* mouths? They did not shut their mouths *to* him? I have seen your Pharisees. They are quite important, aren't they, in their own eyes and also the eyes of others? Your Rabbi must have been very great to shut their mouths *for* them."

"He was."

"So, for one that great, what else was his life like in between a great birth and then death? Was he like the

Roman gods, who enjoy themselves greatly? Or my own Egyptian gods, who work to ensure that they are held in honor amongst their own brethren? Was he in search of more pleasure, or more worship from his followers?"

Pilpos remained grave. "Neither. He served all that he came in contact with. When there was a great crowd listening to his teaching, and the sun began to set, he asked those of us who were closest to him to feed the crowd. May he forgive me, I thought he was mad. That crowd was so great, it would have filled many of the villages in the area, and he wanted us to find food for all of them. One little boy had barely enough fish and bread for his own lunch, but he gave it to my Rabbi. We all thought that at least *he* would have some lunch, but it still didn't solve our problem of feeding a town's worth of people. However, my Rabbi broke a small loaf and handed off the pieces. I broke off a crumb before handing it to Bar-Talmai who was next to me, then another crumb off of the next one that my Rabbi handed me, then off of the next…I lost count of how many bits of bread I was handed, but there had only been five loaves to begin with, he must have broken each into several pieces.

"You know how a rock thrown into a smooth lake makes ripples? That is what it was like; all through that crowd, there were ripples of people breaking off bites of bread or fish and passing it on, but instead of the ripples getting weaker the farther out they go, these ripples grew greater. We were sent to collect the leftovers around the edges of the crowd, and we each collected a full basket's worth. Twelve baskets of bread and fish, left over from five loaves and two fish, after that great crowd of people had all eaten. And my rabbi had done nothing except give thanks to the Father, and share with us."

Bebagin had enjoyed this story, and found himself grinning. "That was a wonderful work. To have such power, and use it for the good of others...it would indicate great kindness. In Egypt, it is our duty to feed the gods. They do not feed us. Even here in Rome, the closest any god got to feeding the people was Minerva, and she only gave the olive tree. The people still have to work, yes? And now I am feeding the *Lares*, to the dismay of Mahdi, there. He would prefer we not offer so many figs." Bebagin waited to see if Mahdi would react, but he got nothing from his chariot driver. The man might as well have been a statue, except for those tiny movements in his wrists. Bebagin smiled and turned back to Pilipos.

"So, your Rabbi used great power to be kind. That would have made quite an impression on the people, I assume. Did your Rabbi then stand up and accept the crowd's worship?"

"No, he sent us out in a boat and he slipped away to be alone with his Father. The crowd was confused. They were ready to make him king then and there, but he was gone and after a while, most of them wandered away to their own homes."

"He did not accept rule over them? This is an odd Rabbi of yours, Pilipos. Aren't the Jews looking for a king to help them get rid of the Romans?"

"Yes, many are. However, Messiah Yeshua did not come to rule the Kingdom of Israel, but to establish a heavenly kingdom on earth."

"Excellent. My Pharoah, also, is a king in the heavens, or so he says. But he rules from his palace in Napata. Where exactly is the center of this heavenly kingdom of your Messiah Yeshua?"

"In the hearts and souls of those who love him."

"Not over by a lake or within a new city or by some holy mountain?"

"No--although I still love the Temple and the Synagogue. But Messiah's Kingdom is wherever his people are, in their midst, and could even be here in this chariot."

Bebagin smiled as he thought of the two bald men in front of him making a kingdom with himself. It was an amusing idea, but he decided to treat Pilipos with gravity and not let his humor take the upper hand.

"Having an opportunity to take the worship and following of people, but turning away from it for the sake of a better one could indicate great wisdom. Or maybe great foolishness, but either way, I am so glad that you appeared by my chariot, Pilipos, and that I get to hear the tale. This truly is a very good tale. At the Candace's palace, I have a room just for my idols and scrolls, and members of the household, great and common alike, come to hear the tales."

Pilipos did not return Bebagin's smile, nor did he seem flattered that the story of his Rabbi would take place next to the stories of the Egyptian or Roman gods. After considering Bebagin for a quiet moment, he asked "Why do you seek so many idols and their tales?"

Bebagin waved one hand in the air. "Oh, it is good to have something to believe in. Men long for immortality, and most often that comes through their family line. As long as a man's son and his son's sons remember him, he will live and continue to have importance. For those such as Mahdi and myself, though, there will be no sons, and we must find our immortality through the kindness of whatever god will listen. My heart is stirred by these stories. The beauty and glory in them--it all hints at what might be true, what must be true. Perhaps, if I learn them all, I can grasp the greatest truth and gain glory for myself. So...I serve my Candace, and through her I serve the great Pharaoh, and I travel and learn of the gods of many peoples, and learn of how to worship them all."

"But do you believe in any yourself?"

"Myself? Oh, yes. All. I believe in them all, and I believe in none. The stories stir my heart, but sometimes the reality that we can see and touch leaves a lack. You see, even great Pharaoh, he is a god, yes? He is the son of Ra himself, and yet he still poops in a pot like the slave who scrapes the ashes. And sometimes the great Pharaoh even grunts as he poops.

"And Caesar, who rules over your people, is he not also a god? But yet I myself have seen the glorious Augustus eat until he vomited, and then eat more. Caesar still stumbles when he's drunk. But I bow before him and offer incense at his temple to worship him. And then I meet with his officials and negotiate trade contracts. But the history of the *Lares* that I recently acquired gives me a little--just a little--joy. So I still believe.

"And now your Rabbi...he may have been great and kind and wise. He may have done some things that no one can explain. He may have had great claims about his parentage. But….did he howl like a beast when the Romans got that cross up and in place?   The Romans are not gentle. No….in truth, one feels that they enjoy breaking the bodies of those they rule over. Did your rabbi lose control of his bowels when he stared death right in the face?"

Pilipos watched the road pass by beneath him for a moment. His voice was almost too low for Bebagin to hear him. "When my Rabbi died, the sky became dark and the earth shook."

Bebagin paused once more. His silence got Mahdi to turn around; rarely was the Overseer ever this quiet. Now this bald Hebrew had made him speechless twice. It was with a noticeable effort that Bebagin swallowed and cleared his throat.

"You said this was two years ago?"

"Yes."

"Now...I do remember that. The prophets and magicians of the Candace's court were stilled. They had no prophecies to utter, but they crouched down and pulled cloaks over their heads. It is not kind to talk of their whimpering, but it is truthful. That darkness was not something any of them could explain. Nothing came of it, so we dismissed it as a sudden cloud that no one saw coming--or going, for that matter. But that darkness attended the death of your Rabbi, here? Was that why your priests at your Temple were unsettled when recounting other darknesses?"

Pilipos drew his eyebrows together. "It may have been. I prefer not to discuss the priests."

Bebagin shook his head. "So, this Rabbi of yours, this 'Son of Man,' he had a bright star at his birth and great darkness at his death. And you continue to claim that he came back to life?"

"He did. We saw him, and he lives yet."

Bebagin continued to roll these thoughts about in his head, and searched for a way to make sense of stories like this that he could almost touch for himself. After another moment, he straightened his back a bit more, and when he spoke, he caught himself using the same voice that fit nicely in his room with his idols and his scrolls and an audience to regale.

"I, too, know of gods who were killed and brought back to life. Osiris had a very loyal wife who used great power to bring him back. As I said, he is now the god of the underworld, and the one whom I must keep appeased. I want to have as great favor in the afterlife as I do now. Who was the magician that brought back your Rabbi?"

Pilipos smiled a bit. "No one. We were all hiding from both the Jews and the Romans, when women brought word. Messiah Yeshua had such goodness, and such power on his own, that death could not conquer him. He entered death as one who had no sin, and he conquered it. There is no power that can separate him from those he loves. He became Lord over death, and now he lives with true, unconquerable life."

"That is better than being the god of the Underworld only."

"It is."

Bebagin's voice became quieter.

"These...these are great things you are telling me, Pilipos the son of God, and it almost seems to be greater than the tales I have shared at the palace…"

"It is greater, because it is no tale but actual truth. Those who saw are writing it all down to make sure the things that we observed with our own eyes are reliably recorded. We saw Messiah Yeshua die, we saw him in the tomb, we saw that tomb empty and the Roman soldiers who had been placed as guards frightened away--"

"The guards were gone?"

Pilipos nodded.

"Yet, it would be death for a Roman soldier to leave his position. And they are well trained and able to stand watch over a silent tomb!

"This tomb was not silent. Things greater than either the guard's training or ability happened there."

"Nobody observed the rising of Osiris. We only tell the tale."

"Many have observed the Messiah. T'omah even poked his finger into the wounds--both the wounds in his hands from the nails and the wound in his side from the spear. They were healing, but still fresh. Messiah Yeshua's living blood pulsed within."

Bebagin had nothing to say. He watched the road, he watched Mahdi's back, which was straight and still and not communicative, he turned and looked about while he thought of the ancient story of Osiris and the modern, seemingly real things he was hearing about. His eyes focused on a cairn that was now significantly behind them, and he swiveled forward to poke Mahdi in the back.

"Mahdi, we should have stopped and offered our figs to the *Lares*. You drove right past, and now I suppose it is too late to turn about and go back...and yet, those again are but tales that we have heard, but that none have witnessed." He turned to Pilipos, and frowned. Bebagin was not used to frowning, and in the back of his mind his consternation surprised even himself.

"So, you attest that the things in my scroll were no mere tales like every country has, but prophecies of a different sort, and you yourself witnessed the truth of it?"

Pilipos nodded.

"And the sacrifice that this Messiah Yeshua demands? I was offering figs to the *Lares* to seek a pleasant journey, until Mahdi grew jealous of the figs. What kind of worship does your risen Rabbi ask for?"

"None but a circumcised heart."

"And how, exactly, is that accomplished? No man can allow his chest to be opened and have a layer of his heart removed….he would not survive. Or is that one of your Rabbi's miracles? Does he regularly bring back those who are sacrificed to him?"

Pilipos grunted slightly, and Bebagin realized that was his way of laughing. "We are already dead. Our sins have killed us. Our idolatry" and he gently tapped the chest beneath him, "separates us from God, and there is no life apart from him. The way that Messiah Yeshua walked alive on the ground and was able to be touched after he had been dead proved that he is in complete control over unseen realms, and the circumcision of the heart is done by his Spirit. No knives are needed. With this circumcision, life comes. We have a practice of water baptism to honor the differentiation between the old, living death, and the new life that comes with understanding about the life in our Messiah. But it is merely an outward sign of what has already happened to the innermost man, the heart and spirit of him."

Bebagin glanced down at the scroll which still rested in his lap. It was partially open and he read the visible portion out loud. "...by the knowledge of himself shall my righteous servant justify many; and he shall bear their iniquities….This is what you mean, Pilipos of God? Knowing of your Rabbi *is* the act of worship? Allowing a spiritual circumcision is the offering? And the only proof...it is this act of baptism?"

Pilipos shrugged. "A circumcised heart would offer its own proof many times as life continues and circumstances allow. But yes, there is no offering such as figs to be left at a cairn, or even the sacrifice of a lamb at a temple...none like those are needed. Messiah Yeshua was the great offering for all time."

Bebagin felt full of questions, and had a difficult time finding exactly which one he wanted to ask. "I have much I wish to know about this Rabbi, this Messiah Yeshua. Other tales are beautiful but shrouded in mystery. They change between tellers. This one feels as real as the stones in the road. I suspect there are actual answers to my questions."

"There are. You may ask as many questions as you desire."

Bebagin glanced down once more at the scroll. "It says he shall justify many and bear their iniquities. Justify to who?"

Pilipos nodded. "To his own Father, the Almighty."

"Almighty is a great title."

"It is."

"Many gods are proclaimed as mighty, but no, none of them could really deserve the title of almighty, although flattery is often used. Osiris could not raise himself, and now he is god of the underworld only. The *Lares* that I have acquired have very limited influence. So, your Messiah makes a god who claims to be almighty feel that his believers are justified….and their iniquities, then?'

"Because he had no iniquities of his own, when Messiah Yeshua gave himself up to be crucified, he made space for all the iniquities of any who come to him. All of my sins, the sins of my brothers and sisters in the Messiah, died with him. But when he came back to life, the sins stayed dead. There is nothing left to keep Ha Shem, the Almighty God, from looking upon us with his full favor."

Bebagin thought of the many ways he had tried to curry favor with gods and rulers through his life. To be sure, for the most part he had been successful, and that was why he was now well-dressed, and riding in a good chariot. But his life was a result of careful, conscientious posturing towards those who could hurt him as easily as honor him. What would it be like if he knew the Candace was always in a favorable mood, and pleased with him at all times? For that matter, what would it have been like if it had been his father who looked upon him with favor instead of sternness?

He smiled gently at Pilipos. "The full favor of a fully powerful god would be worth everything. It would change everything."

"It would. It has." The simple security in Pilipos's voice caused Bebagin's heart to feel expansive, and he took several deep breaths to explore that new space. No other story had ever affected him so. He was not quite sure what to do with his feelings.

"It seems, Pilipos, son of God, that every question I ask makes me wonder more things. I suspect that my questions might become as infinite as your God's power." A shimmer up ahead along the road prompted Bebagin's thoughts. "And yet, while I have questions, my own heart feels like it is shining….shining right out of my chest. It is as if dead layers have already been removed. You say that baptism is the sign of understanding? Is it only in a sacred river? Your Rabbi lived along the Jordan, did he not? Is that where baptisms for your Messiah are accomplished?"

"Just as sacrifices in the Temple are no longer necessary, no single river or lake is the only correct place."

"There is water ahead; is that water suitable for a baptism according to your Rabbi?"

"It is."

Bebagin paused. His thoughts were rushing so fast that he could hardly comprehend them. All that he had heard flowed around and away like water itself, breaking onto rocks of memory, then bounding over a precipice to a depth that he did not understand. He remembered the crinkled nose of the slave who carried Pharoah's pot out of the royal bedchamber in the morning; he thought of the slaves who supported Caesar as he was nearly dragged away from a feast table to his private rooms, where none could witness the indignity that heavy drink had brought upon him. He noticed moldering bread and fruit as Mahdi drove doggedly past yet another cairn, not even slowing the horses. He let all that he had heard from Pilipos carry him to the thought of a Rabbi standing in a tomb with fresh wounds, so full of his own life and joy that he had overcome death by his very being.

Bebagin felt those thoughts of this Rabbi carry him right over that precipice, and his spirit fell--or was he flying?--like a cataract of the Nile into the understanding of how much greater this real man was than even the most astounding tales of Osiris.

"If there is water, why should I not be baptized, O Pilipos who is a son of God? Is there any reason why an Ethiopian eunuch should not have his heart circumcised, and learn to live in the understanding of these great events?"

Pilipos looked sternly into Bebagin's face. For the first time in a long time, Bebagin felt that he was in a position underneath someone who was much greater and wiser than he. He allowed Pilipos to search, as it seemed, into his very mind.

"This is no mere tale."

"I understand."

"A circumcised heart changes everything you think and say and do; you will not be the same, nor will you be able to desire the same kinds of power or prestige."

"Hmm. That would seem a natural outcome if a heart has been completely changed."

"And Messiah Yeshua does not stand next to idols."

"What need would there be to ask for favor from idols, if I am able to stand under the full favor of an almighty God? If there were nothing in myself that offended a greater God, there would be no point in begging for the aid of statues that may not have any life beyond their stone faces. "

"You cannot live as you have done before."

"Of course not. A living God that truly interacts with His people would change how all things worked."

"Do you understand that the Messiah Yeshua is truly the living God?"

"I understand that the testimony of this old prophet of the Jews became real. I believe that your testimony of what you saw yourself is dependable. Do not you Jews have a legal code that accepts as correct anything that can be testified to by two or more witnesses? In addition, my own heart has taken flight, like the mighty waters of the Nile leaping over the cataracts. I have never experienced such a thing. I wish to be baptized and have this circumcised heart, and to tell a better story at home--a real story."

Pilipos turned towards Mahdi, but did not poke him. Instead, he rested a hand on the charioteer's shoulder, and asked quietly "Would you stop, my brother?"

Bebagin nearly choked. "Your brother?"

Pilpos's grin was huge under that beard. "As you come to Messiah Yeshua and are adopted, not as a servant but a son of God, all who have been similarly adopted become your brothers. Mahdi was called by the Spirit to the Messiah not long ago, but has already learned so much. He might be able to continue to instruct you, if I am not."

Bebagin could not see much of Mahdi's bald head beneath his turban and scarf, but he noticed that the horses stumbled a bit as Mahdi directed them closer to the shore nearby. They were abruptly stopped; out of character for the skilled charioteer, and Bebagin peered around to the side of Mahdi's face. "For how long?"

Mahdi kept his eyes fixed firmly on the reins in his hands. "For several weeks, Overseer."

"So, while I was reading, did you already know the words of this prophecy?"

"No, Overseer. That was new to me. I have heard much of the history of Messiah Yeshua. I worked very hard to commit it to memory. I can share the words with you as you wish."

Bebagin nearly slapped the man on his back as he laughed, but restrained himself at the last moment. "Ha! That would be a reversal! I have always been the one with the tales, and now perhaps it is time for me to only listen and learn! Well, you will need to talk much more than usual, Mahdi, if you have learned such a great deal of this Rabbi. And I will perhaps need to talk much less."

Bebagin stood and gathered his robes about him. His foot nudged the bag of figs as he moved to step down. "Hmm. Mahdi, is that why you were so reluctant to stop and offer figs at the cairns? Because you have already chosen belief in this Messiah?"

He was in a position now to see Mahdi flush under his dark skin. "No, Overseer. I just...I like figs."

Bebagin continued to chuckle as he followed Pilipos to the edge of the water. He chuckled as he pulled off his outer robes and his tunic. He chose not to look in Mahdi's direction, not caring what the charioteer thought of seeing the great Overseer of the Candace's treasury in a disrobed and undignified manner. The great cataract of joy that had begun to rush like water in his heart continued to grow in strength as he answered questions from Pilipos, and allowed himself to be lowered under the water. For a brief second, he opened his eyes and saw the shimmer on the surface above him, the shadow that was the man supporting his back, and he allowed that flowing water in his heart meet the water of the lake. There was joy within and joy without, and as he came back up into the air, he felt like he had never drawn breath before. Being so very alive felt new, and he lifted his hands as he shook the water from his eyes and hair. The sun sparkled on each drop as it flew away from him, and shimmered on the surface of the water.

As he continued to squint and shake, that shimmer grew, and when Bebagin had cleared his eyes, he could not find Pilipos. Bebagin turned in a few directions, then shot a look at Mahdi in question. The charioteer opened his eyes wide, and if he'd had eyebrows they would have been raised high on his forehead. Mahdi then shrugged and spread his hands out, palm upwards as he responded to Bebagin's unvoiced question. "I do not know, Overseer. He was there, then the sun on the water as you came up was bright, and I could not see…."

Bebagin chuckled again leaving the water, as he had chuckled on his way in. "Well, a real and living God can do many things, can he not, Mahdi? We have much to discuss, and it seems I have much to learn and not so much to tell. Yet. I am sure that as I get to know this Messiah Yeshua who has real life in him, I will eventually be able to tell many things. Let us simply continue on, and perhaps this time I will stand by you and you can tell me what you have learned….my brother."

Mahdi was silent, and Bebagin wondered if his normally quiet driver would need poking to get him to talk. But as Bebagin stepped in the chariot and deposited his bundled robes on his former seat, Mahdi stepped to the side the way he had for Pilipos. For the first time in his life, his eyes met

Bebagin's. "I would be glad to tell you more of our Savior, brother."

Mahdi's skill was perfect as he coaxed the horses back into motion and onto the road. Neither he nor the Overseer cared that they left behind a small trunk, open and lopsided in the edge of the lake where the small waves washed in and out around several small statues.

ENDNOTES

It feels like it is a rather perilous thing to write stories about someone so very real and so very alive as Jesus. I have wanted to portray him accurately, and to stay true to the account we have in Scripture, while also keeping historical and cultural details as true as possible, so that in these stories we can get a fresh sense for how good our Savior is. That said, I am neither a Biblical nor an archaeological scholar, and while I did my best to research well and make sure details were authentic, I'm sure I've missed the mark here and there. I hope you're able to just enjoy these stories and feel like you've glimpsed a bit of the world that our Jesus really did move through. I'm so grateful that you have read my little book, and my greatest hope is that it helped you love God just a little bit more.

It would not be overstating a single blessed thing to say that this little book exists largely because of the community of the Rabbit Room. I have found such encouragement there to do the work of creating stories that needed to be told. In addition, the sub-group of Writing Rabbits has been instrumental, and even more particularly, the feedback from Ashley, Natalie, and Christina has been a blessing. Thank you so much, my friends.

I am blessed to call Michelle both my friend and my editor. Michelle, both the times you were "not gentle," and the times that you told me something was beautiful were life-giving. Thank you for working with me.

My husband and kids have put up with a fair bit while I labored to bring this into existence, and I hope they know how much I love them and how grateful I am for their hugs.

One thing that I enjoyed hugely during the writing of these stories was discovering some Hebrew names and words that were new to me.   I relied heavily upon the Hebrew Names Bible, available through Blue Letter Bible.

Midwife

A couple of years ago, I decided to watch the livestream for Andrew Peterson's concert "Behold the Lamb of God." I was enjoying it immensely right up to the point where Jill Philips started singing "A Labor of Love," and got to the lines "Little Mary, full of grace, with the tears upon her face...and no mother's hand to hold." Those lines still just shatter me. I couldn't help wondering why on earth Mary had to be alone...midwives were so common then, and as a doula, the idea of a new mother birthing all by herself just killed me. So, my apologies to Andrew, but I needed a better story for Mary. This started some fascinating research into ancient Roman midwifery practices (easier to Google than "Ancient Hebrew midwifery practices during the Roman occupation"), a few traditional stories told around the Nativity that were new to me, and some speculation as to why a stable and not the inn was available.

(And that song, "Labor of Love," is absolutely beautiful and everyone should listen to the album or watch the annual concert, or both.)

Return

If the idea of lions ravaging the Samaritan countryside was new to you, as it was to me, check out 2 Kings 17:24-34. The whole story is there, and for me it explained a lot about why the Samarian region was looked down upon by the rest of Israel.

Understand

The passages that Bebagin read out loud to Mahdi are from Isaiah 53, and Pilipos quotes Isaiah 7:14. All Scripture verses are from the Hebrew Names Bible, offered generously by the good people at BlueLetterBible.org

The Stories are True.
S.D.G.

ABOUT THE AUTHOR

C. Rochelle lives in the gloriously drippy Pacific Northwest with her husband Jeff, Zeke the cat, Walter the dog, and a harp (whose name is not public knowledge). After homeschooling her three now-grown children, C. Rochelle is finally starting to bring out the stories that have been tumbling about inside her head for decades. When not bringing new stories into the world, she works as a birth doula to help women bring new humans into the world.